**Other books by Jane Cutler
featuring Edward and Jason Fraser
with pictures by Tracey Campbell Pearson**

### No Dogs Allowed

★ What Ramona is to Beezus, Edward Fraser is to his older brother, Jason, and readers who like [Beverly] Cleary's characters will find these siblings just as much fun . . . In five chapters the boys learn how to swim, visit the country, and raise money—common events that become laugh-aloud treats in Cutler's capable hands.　　　—STARRED/*Booklist*

### Rats!

★ What makes these stories so inviting and funny is Cutler's exceptional talent for describing events from the boys' rather literal point of view . . . The author's wonderful sense of timing and the cadence and symmetry of her language make this a natural title for reading aloud.

　　　　　　　　　—STARRED/*School Library Journal*

# 'Gator Aid

A Sunburst Book ★ Farrar Straus Giroux

JANE CUTLER

# 'Gator Aid

Pictures by Tracey Campbell Pearson

Library of Congress Cataloging-in-Publication Data
Cutler, Jane.
    'Gator aid / Jane Cutler ; pictures by Tracey Campbell Pearson. —
1st ed.
        p.   cm.
    Summary: Imaginative second-grader Edward swears he saw a baby
alligator in the Shaw Park lake, but no one believes him.
    ISBN 0-374-42521-0 (pbk.)
    [1. Alligators—Fiction.  2. Animals—Infancy—Fiction.]   I. Pearson,
Tracey Campbell, ill.  II. Title.
PZ7.C985Gat  1999
[Fic]—dc21

                                                            98-49033

*For Fran Stone*
—J.C.

*For Adam and Alex*
—T.C.P.

# Contents

# 'Gator Aid

# Duck!

Edward Fraser crept up to his brother Jason's half-closed bedroom door. In a low, threatening voice he said, "Tick. Tock. Tick. Tock. Tick. Tock."

Jason was playing air-guitar, watching himself in the mirror.

"Tick-tock, tick-tock, tick-tock," Edward insisted.

"It's 'Tick. Tick. Tick. Tick,'" said Jason. He pushed the door shut with his foot.

Edward made a face at the closed door. Then he advanced menacingly on his hands and knees down the hallway and into the kitchen, where his mother stood, looking undecided.

"Tick-tick-tick-tick," he threatened.

Quickly, Mrs. Fraser grabbed a wooden spoon and pulled the sleeve of her sweater over her hand so only the spoon showed. "Avast, ye lubbers, it's the crocodile!" she cried, waving the spoon in the air. "He's et me hand and liked the taste of it so much, he wants to eat the rest of me. And all because of Peter Pan!"

She kicked off her shoes and jumped onto a chair. "Hide me from the croc," she commanded, "lest every one of ye wants to feel the stroke of me hook!" She waved her spoon at a band of invisible pirates.

Edward stopped ticking and stood up. "That spoon doesn't make a very good hook, Mom," he said.

His mother got off the chair and slipped her shoes back on. "It makes as good a hook as you make a crocodile," she answered. "It's all pretend, isn't it?"

"Well, yes," Edward said. "But the play was pretend, too, and Captain Hook had a real hook."

"A real *pretend* hook," his mother reminded him.

Edward shrugged. "I know. But it seemed real in the play."

"Except that you know Arnie Pollock doesn't have a hook instead of a hand, right?"

"Yeah," Edward agreed. "But what I mean is, while I was watching the play, it all seemed real. Including the hook."

"That's good," Mrs. Fraser said. "It means the fifth-graders did their job. When you put on a play, you're supposed to make it seem real.

"Of course, the people watching a play have a job to do, too," she added.

"I know," said Edward. "Mr. Fortney told us. The audience has to sit still and be quiet." Mr. Fortney was teaching second grade this year. Edward liked him, but not quite as much as he had when he was Jason's teacher.

"The audience does have to sit still and be quiet," said Mrs. Fraser. "But there's more. Did Mr. Fortney tell you anything else the audience needs to remember?"

"Yep," Edward recalled. "No poking."

"Anything else?" his mother asked hopefully.

Edward thought. "Nope. That's it. That's what the audience is supposed to do."

"Well, there is something else," Mrs. Fraser said. "And it's important. But maybe Mr. Fortney decided it was too hard for second-graders to understand."

6

Edward was interested. "What is it?"

"The people watching a play are supposed to 'suspend disbelief,' " his mother said.

"Suspend?" asked Edward.

"Suspend means 'stop for a while.' "

"Disbelief?" asked Edward.

"Not-believing," explained his mother.

"Stop not-believing for a while?" puzzled Edward. "I think Mr. Fortney was right," he decided. "It's too hard for second-graders to understand."

Mrs. Fraser tried again. "It's not really that hard. It just means that people need to go to a play willing to believe that everything they see on stage is real. Until the play is over, of course."

"No squirming, no talking, no poking, and no disbelieving," said Edward.

"Right," his mother said.

"It would take an awful lot of not-believing for anyone to believe that wooden spoon you're holding is Captain Hook's hook," said Edward, getting back to his point.

Mrs. Fraser frowned at the spoon. "You're probably right," she agreed. She pushed her hand back out of her sleeve and began to look undecided again.

"Can I ride my bike over to the park?" Edward asked.

"May I," his mother corrected.

"Sure, if you're not busy," Edward cracked.

"Edward, stop that," Mrs. Fraser said.

"Well, can I?"

"May I."

Edward gave in. "May I?"

"Yes, you may. And don't forget to wear your helmet."

"I won't."

"And walk your bike when you cross the street."

"I will."

"And come home before it starts to get dark."

"Okay."


It was the Monday of spring vacation, and after all the excitement of the fifth grade's performance of *Peter Pan* the night before, Jason was feeling let down. But he was feeling relieved, too.

He'd had enough of *Peter Pan*. He'd had enough of the theater. He'd certainly had enough of Ms. Bascombe, his fifth-grade teacher, running around with three pencils sticking out of her piled-up red hair, saying things like "The play's the thing!" and "There's no business like show business!"

Ms. Bascombe had been an actress before she became a schoolteacher. The theater, she claimed, was in her blood.

Anyway, *Peter Pan* was over. And Jason, who had played the part of a timid pirate named Smee, was glad. Putting on a play was the hardest work anyone in the fifth grade had ever done. So many details. So many things to remember. And so much to organize and coordinate.

It had been fun at the very end, Jason had to admit, to stand behind the footlights and bow while the audience clapped. And he was glad the performance went well, and that even Lucas Larraby remembered his lines.

The cast party was fun, too. Pizza and soda, everyone tired and happy, and Ms. Bascombe telling them they could all be stars if they wanted to be.

Jason wanted to be a star, all right. But not a star who acted in plays. Jason wanted to be a rock star. He wanted to play loud music on an electric guitar, with a bass player and a drummer. He wanted to holler "Crank it up!" until the music was so loud it filled the whole stadium, or wherever he was playing. Of course, he would have to get special earplugs, like real musicians had. And he would have to learn to play the guitar.

Jason wandered into the kitchen. "What are you cooking?" he asked his mother.

"Nothing," she said. "What are you doing?"

"Nothing," said Jason, opening the refrigerator door and staring at the almost-empty shelves.

"It sounded to me like you were playing air-guitar," Mrs. Fraser said.

"I was," said Jason.

"That was a joke, Jason," his mother told him. "You can't hear someone playing air-guitar."

"Funny," he said.

Mrs. Fraser saw that Jason was grumpy. She tried to cheer him up. "Well, it's okay for you to play air-guitar, I guess, just as long as you don't get interested in playing air-drums, too."

Jason wondered what the difference would be between air-guitar and air-drums. "Why not?" he asked.

"Why not what?" his mother replied.

"Why isn't it okay for me to play air-drums?"

"Drums are entirely too noisy, Jason," said his mother.

"Air-drums?" queried Jason.

"All drums," she said firmly.

Jason shook his head and closed the refrigerator door. "There's nothing to eat," he said.

"I know," said Mrs. Fraser as she walked out of the kitchen. "I should go to the market, but I just can't get into the mood. I think I'll play air-market. And then we can have air-dinner. What do you think?"

"What do I think about what?" said Jason.

"What do you think about air-dinner, for a change?" said Mrs. Fraser.

"Whatever," muttered Jason, frowning to himself and wondering what his mother thought they were talking about.

Edward strapped on his bike helmet and rode up the driveway. He walked his bike across three quiet intersections between the Frasers' house and the park. Edward thought this was a silly rule. Not many cars came up or down these streets. And one was a dead end with so little traffic that Rooter, the Friedmans' old black Lab, took his naps right in the middle of it every single day. Or did, Edward remembered, until he got lost last week.

Edward had forgotten about Rooter. Everyone in the neighborhood was supposed to be keeping an eye out for him. Rooter was old, and he had the worst case of doggy breath anyone had ever smelled. But the Friedmans loved him. They were worried about him and wanted him back. And Edward was worried about him, too. He had just let it slip his mind.

"Here, Rooter," he called. "Here, boy!" He looked all around, but no old, gray-muzzled dog came limping toward him.

Since it was spring vacation and all the kids in the neighborhood had plenty of time on their hands, maybe they could organize themselves into search-and-rescue teams. He would have to talk to Jason about it. No, not crabby old Jason. He'd talk to Alexander Friedman and Elaine Abrams and Andrew Kelly. And if they wanted to talk to Jason, they could. But as far as Edward was concerned, Jason could spend his whole vacation in his room, playing air-guitar.

Edward had tried playing air-guitar. It was no fun at all. What in the world had come over Jason? Maybe the theater had gotten into his blood, the way it had into Ms. Bascombe's. Maybe Jason was never going to be his old self again.

When Edward got to the park, he locked up his helmet and his bike in the bike rack. Then he stood with his hands in his back pockets and looked around to see who was doing what.

It was quiet. Brittany Chan's grandfather was sitting in the open-sided sun shelter chatting and playing Go with Emily Han's uncle. Two old men Edward didn't know were silently concentrating on a game of chess.

In the sandbox that was built around the small slides and the baby swings, a few toddlers with their mothers or their baby-sitters keeping an eye on them were playing in the sand.

Edward watched one toddler carefully shoveling sand into a blue plastic bucket with a yellow plastic shovel. He watched another toddler crawling around making motor noises and shoving a big toy dump truck ahead of him. He saw a shy toddler with a big green pacifier in her mouth watching the others play. Then he saw a baby sitting with his legs stretched out to give him balance. The baby was eating sand.

Everything at the park was in order. Everything was exactly as Edward expected it to be.

He walked through the bright green new grass toward the lake on the other side of the soccer field.

Down by the water, he saw Jeffrey Sanders, Tyler Franklin, and Alexander Friedman with the twins Marlene and Marilyn Conroy. Alexander had a stick in his hand. He was trying to poke the big turtles lined up on a log, head to tail, like cars in a traffic jam. But the stick wasn't long enough.

The turtles lay perfectly still. Their heads and their legs stuck out of their shells. They were the same black-brown color as the log, and they seemed to feel perfectly safe. Even when Alexander hit the water with the stick, not one of them so much as blinked.

A family of ducks—father, mother, and six fluffy brown babies—swam in circles farther away from the shore. The park's two white swans glided peacefully near the small overgrown island in the middle of the lake. And even though he couldn't see her, Edward could hear Miss Lucy, the cantankerous goose, scolding and complaining over on the opposite shore.

"Hey, here's Edward," said Tyler. "Now we've got enough people to play a good game of hide-and-seek."

"All *right!*" said Alexander. He dropped the stick and wiped his muddy hands on his jeans.

"Let's go!" said Jeffrey.

"We don't want to play hide-and-seek," said Marlene.

"You don't?" said Jeffrey. "You said you did, before."

"Well, we don't now," said Marilyn.

"Now we want to play I-spy," said Marlene.

"I-spy is the same as hide-and-seek," said Rudy.

"Is not," Marlene and Marilyn said together.

"Is too," said Alexander.

"Not," said Marilyn.

"Too," said Tyler.

"Not," said Marlene.

"Too!" yelled Jeffrey.

"What do you want to play, Edward?" said Marlene. "Do you want to play hide-and-seek, or do you want to play I-spy?"

"Yes, Edward," said Marilyn, "which do you choose?"

Edward thought. He wasn't sure. It didn't matter. It was almost exactly the same game. Just the words were different. He frowned and squinched his eyes and tried to look as if he were thinking.

"Marlene," said Marilyn, "do we have any of those chocolate-marshmallow Easter eggs left? The ones Granny sent that Mom said we didn't have to save for our baskets?"

"Why, yes, Marilyn," said Marlene. "We do have a few of those especially delicious eggs left."

"If Edward decides he wants to play I-spy," Marilyn said, "we could give him some."

"What a good idea, Marilyn," Marlene said. "I was wondering what in the world we were going to do with the rest of those yummy milk-chocolate and marshmallow eggs. I know I couldn't eat another one."

"Me neither," said Marilyn. She gazed up at the sky. She waited. Nobody said anything. Edward tried to look as if he were still thinking hard. "Of course, if Edward would rather play hide-and-seek . . ." said Marilyn.

"I wouldn't!" Edward interrupted. "I've decided. I want to play I-spy!"

"All right, all right," said Tyler, "let's just play something before it gets too late."

"Yeah," said Jeffrey.

"Yeah," said Alexander.

"This tree is home base," said Marilyn.

"And you're It!" said Marlene, tagging Edward and darting away.

"Me?" he cried. "Why me?"

" 'Cause I tagged you!" Marlene said, laughing.

"You're It, Edward," said Jeffrey. "Start counting."

Edward folded his arms against the tree and rested his forehead on them. He closed his eyes. He heard the other kids running away. He felt lonely. Edward always felt lonely when he played hide-and-seek or I-spy. He felt lonely if he was It, and he felt lonely if he was hiding.

One time he had such a good hiding place, nobody was able to find him. The game ended, and all the other kids went home. But Edward didn't know that, so he kept on hiding.

It started to get dark and cold. Edward shivered, but he kept hiding. Then he heard his mom and Jason. "Edward," they called, "olly-olly-ox-in-free! Come out, come out, wherever you are!"

"Ninety-eight, ninety-nine, one hundred. Ready or not, here I come!" shouted Edward. He looked around. Nobody. He must not have counted fast enough. Everyone already had found a place to hide.

Slowly, watchfully, Edward sidled away from home base and started toward the grove of small and large trees on the other side of the lake. Someone almost always hid there.

As he stole around the lake, he pretended he was an Indian out hunting in the forest. He walked as quietly as he could, the way an Indian would have walked in his deerskin moccasins. His seeing and his hearing got as sharp as an Indian's as he studied every shadow and strained to hear the slightest sounds. Keen and knowing, the Indian stalked his prey.

"Watch out, Edward!" cried Mr. Fortney when the Indian bumped into him.

"Mr. Fortney!" exclaimed Edward. "What are *you* doing here?"

"I'm trying out my new binoculars," said Mr. Fortney. "My wife gave them to me for my birthday, and this is the first chance I've had to use them."

"What are you looking at?" Edward asked.

"Everything!" said Mr. Fortney happily. "They make things that are far away seem close. Why, I can see things through the binoculars that I could never see with my eyes alone. I plan to use the binoculars for serious bird-watching, when I go on outings with the Audubon Society. But today I'm just fooling around. Want to take a look?" the teacher offered.

Edward sure did. He might be able to spot someone hiding over on the other side of the lake. If he did, he could easily make it back to home base first. Then he'd be finished being It, which was worse, he'd decided, than having to hide.

Mr. Fortney draped the leather strap around Edward's neck and showed him how to adjust the

binoculars. Edward's glasses bumped up against the eyepieces as he focused the lenses.

"Wow! I can see everything! These are great!" Edward exclaimed as he scanned the lakeshore and the island in the middle of the lake with the powerful binoculars.

Mr. Fortney looked proud.

Carefully, Edward searched for someone hiding or the shadow of someone hiding. He got ready to call out, "I spy So-and-so behind a tree!" He would hand the binoculars back to Mr. Fortney and race for home base.

There! Something moved! Who was it? He had to be sure so he could call out the right name, or else it wouldn't count.

"I spy . . ." Edward said to himself.

"Excuse me?" said Mr. Fortney.

"I spy . . ." Edward repeated.

"Pardon?" said Mr. Fortney.

"I spy—a crocodile!" exclaimed Edward, as the shadow he'd been watching slipped into the water.

"I spy a crocodile!" he exclaimed again. "Mr. Fortney, there's a crocodile in the lake!"

"Good try, Edward," Mr. Fortney said pleasantly. "For a second there, I actually believed you!"

Edward quickly handed the binoculars to Mr.

Fortney. "I'm not kidding!" he said. "Here, look for yourself. Right over there!" Edward pointed to the spot.

Mr. Fortney took back the binoculars, held them up to his eyes, and studied the place Edward pointed to. "Do you see it?" Edward asked excitedly.

"Oh, I sure do," teased Mr. Fortney. "I see it clearly. It's black, and it's at least ten feet long." He smiled at Edward.

"No, it's not!" Edward protested. "It's brown and it has yellow stripes around it. And it's not very long at all."

"That wouldn't be a crocodile, then, Edward," said Mr. Fortney in his patient teacher way. "That would be a baby alligator."

"It looked like a crocodile!" Edward insisted.

"The stripes," Mr. Fortney explained as he looked back at the spot Edward had pointed to. "The stripes would mean it's an alligator. Baby crocodiles don't have stripes."

"What's the difference?" asked Edward.

"I just told you," said Mr. Fortney.

"I mean, what's the difference between grown alligators and grown crocodiles?" explained Edward.

"Well, not really all that much," answered Mr. Fortney, still peering through his binoculars. "They're both reptiles. They're both fierce. They're both carnivorous."

"What's that?"

"They eat meat."

"What else?" asked Edward.

"They both live in North America. In places like Florida, Louisiana, and North and South Carolina. In swamps and warm streams."

"And lakes," added Edward.

"But not in lakes as cold as this one," said Mr. Fortney. He lowered the binoculars and smiled at Edward again.

"I bet it was that performance of *Peter Pan* that got you interested in crocodiles and alligators, wasn't it?"

Edward didn't answer. He knew it would be rude to contradict his teacher. And he could tell Mr. Fortney didn't believe he'd seen a crocodile *or* an alligator.

"You have a lot of natural curiosity and a lively imagination, Edward," the teacher continued, "and that's good."

"Yes, sir," agreed Edward, trying to look as curious as possible. "Mr. Fortney," he said, "what kind of meat do crocodiles and alligators like to eat?"

"Whatever they can find and catch," said Mr. Fortney. "For example, Edward, if there really were an alligator here at Shaw Park Lake, it might be interested in eating one of those little ducklings." He pointed to the duck family, now swimming in a line. "Well, I better be going now," the teacher said. "It was nice to see you, Edward."

" 'Bye, Mr. Fortney," Edward said, without taking his eyes off the ducks. He was sure they were the same ones he'd seen before. There was the father duck. There was the mother. And swimming in a row behind their parents were the six—no, the *five* fluffy brown babies.

Five?

Five!

# KIDNEWS

Edward rode home as fast as he could. He dropped his bike in the middle of the driveway and rushed into the house and to the family room, where the encyclopedia was.

First he looked up *alligator*. "Found in North Carolina, Florida, and Louisiana," he read. "The young are black or brown with yellow bands."

Then he looked up *crocodile*. "Like an alligator," he read, "but more aggressive, with a narrow snout. In the U.S., lives in the Everglades and the Florida Keys."

Jason stuck his head into the family room. "You left your bike right where Mom could run over it when she comes back from the market. Better put it away," he bossed.

Edward was sitting cross-legged on the floor with the encyclopedia open in his lap. "There's an alligator living in Shaw Park Lake!" he told his brother.

"Sure," Jason said. "Except it's not an alligator. It's a crocodile with a clock in its stomach, and it's looking for Captain Hook."

"Jason," Edward said, "I mean really."

"Me, too," teased Jason, "I mean really, too."

"Jason!" Edward cried.

"Calm down," said Jason. "There can't be an alligator in that lake. Alligators don't live around here. You just have an overactive imagination. That's what Dad says."

"But Jason, I saw it when I looked through Mr. Fortney's binoculars."

"Where?"

"At the park. A little while ago."

"What was Mr. Fortney doing at our park?" Jason wanted to know.

"He was trying out his new binoculars. The ones his wife got him for his birthday. And he let me look through them. And I saw an alligator! I saw it slide into the water and eat a baby duck!" Edward put the encyclopedia aside and imitated the alligator. He crept along the floor, opened his mouth wide, and chomp! he got the duckling.

Jason came on into the room and picked up the encyclopedia. "You saw something in the lake that looked like this?" he asked, pointing to the picture of an alligator.

"Yep," Edward nodded.

"You saw an alligator like this one eat a baby duck?" Jason asked.

Edward hesitated. "Edward," warned Jason, "you did or didn't see an alligator eat a duck at Shaw Park Lake?"

"I did. I mean, I didn't. I mean, first I saw a duck family, a father duck and a mother duck with six babies. Then I saw the alligator. Then I saw the ducks again. And there were only five!"

"Five ducks?" quizzed Jason.

"Five babies," said Edward. "And it was the same family. And they were swimming right near where the alligator slid into the water."

"And you and Mr. Fortney both saw this alligator?" Jason asked. Edward hesitated again. "Edward, did you *and* Mr. Fortney both see the alligator or not?"

"I saw it."

"And what did Mr. Fortney see?"

"How am I supposed to know what Mr. Fortney saw?" bluffed Edward.

"Did he say he saw an alligator?"

Edward looked down. "No," he admitted.

"That's just what I thought," Jason declared. "Dad's right. You have an overactive imagination. Too much *Peter Pan* probably. Kids like you shouldn't even be allowed to go to plays. You can't tell the difference between what's real and what isn't."

"Mom says that's good!" protested Edward. "She says it's part of what people are supposed to do."

"What?" asked Jason.

"Not be able to tell the difference."

"Are you sure that's what Mom said?"

"Yes."

"Well, I think she's wrong. If you can't tell the difference between what's real and what isn't, this is the sort of thing that happens."

"What is?"

"You leave your bike right smack in the middle of the driveway, where Mom could hit it when she comes back," said Jason. "If I were you, I'd move it."

Just then someone rang the doorbell. They rang

it over and over again, impatiently. Jason went to the door and looked through the peephole. He saw it was Marlene and Marilyn Conroy, so he opened the door.

"Where's Edward?" Marlene wanted to know.

"Don't try to hide him," Marilyn warned. "We know he's here. We saw his bike in the driveway."

"Edward's right downstairs," Jason told them. "Why would I try to hide him?"

Marlene and Marilyn headed toward the family room. "*Edward*," they both threatened.

Edward tore past them. "I have to move my bike," he cried as he dashed outside.

Marlene and Marilyn about-faced and followed him. "Hold on, Edward," Marlene said.

"Not so fast, Edward," Marilyn called.

The girls cornered him in the driveway. "Where were you?" demanded Marilyn.

"Where was I?" echoed Edward.

"Where were you when we were playing I-spy and you were supposed to be It?"

"Where was I?" Edward stalled. "Let me think." He put his fist on his forehead, to show the Conroys how hard he was thinking. "Well," he said, "first I was at the tree, with my eyes closed, counting to a hundred while the rest of you hid."

"And then?" said Marlene.

"And then I finished counting and opened my eyes and called 'Ready or not, here I come.' "

"And then?"

"And then I started walking around the lake to the grove of trees on the other side, because I knew somebody probably would be hiding over there."

"And then?"

"Then I met Mr. Fortney. He was trying out a brand-new pair of binoculars his wife gave him for his birthday."

*"And then?"*

"Then he asked if I wanted to try his new binoculars. And I said yes. And then I saw the alligator!"

"And then you saw the what?" exclaimed Marilyn.

"The alligator. The alligator that's living in the lake and eating baby ducks."

"There's an alligator living in Shaw Park Lake?" asked wide-eyed Marlene.

"Yep." Edward nodded.

"There's an alligator living in Shaw Park Lake that's eating ducks?" asked wide-eyed Marilyn.

Edward nodded again.

"And you and Mr. Fortney saw it through his binoculars?"

Edward crossed his fingers behind his back and nodded once more.

"Wow!" the girls exclaimed.

"Wait!" Edward called as they started up the driveway. "Where are you going?"

"Home," said Marilyn.

"To call Janice," said Marlene. "If we can catch her before she goes on the air, she can get the alligator story on KIDNEWS this afternoon."

Janice Conroy was Marilyn and Marlene's older sister. She was in high school and had her own radio show, called KIDNEWS. KIDNEWS was on the air every weekday at 4:55, a five-minute news program especially for kids.

"Janice has a nose for news," the Conroys always bragged.

Edward had asked his mother what they meant. "Oh, it's sort of like a hunting dog with a nose for birds," his mother had explained.

"You mean Janice can smell news?" Edward had asked.

"Something like that," Mrs. Fraser had replied, not looking up from the toaster she was fixing.

"Be sure to listen to KIDNEWS today, Edward," the Conroys called. "Your name might be on the radio!"

"I'll listen," Edward assured them, watching with relief as they hurried off.

Edward put away his bike and his helmet and came back into the house. Jason was restlessly not doing anything. "What was that all about?" he asked.

"Oh, nothing," Edward answered.

"Nothing?" Jason asked.

"Sort of nothing," Edward said.

"That was a big powwow for nothing, Edward."

"Well, see, I accidentally ditched the Conroys and some other kids at the park."

"You accidentally ditched them?"

"You don't think I'd ditch them on purpose, do you?"

Jason didn't answer.

"I just forgot about them," continued Edward. "I got interested in the alligator, and I forgot."

"How could you forget about them?" Jason wanted to know. "Weren't all of you together at the park?"

"They were hiding," Edward explained. "And I was It. Nobody was together."

"You just left them there hiding and came home?" Jason shook his head.

"I didn't mean to forget them, Jason. Honest. I

32

just got excited when I saw the alligator." Edward noticed his brother was looking a little more interested, so he added, "And the duckling."

"Look at me, Edward," Jason said. Edward looked at his brother. "Are you telling the truth? Did you really see an alligator at Shaw Park Lake?"

"I *am* telling the truth," said Edward. "I *did* see an alligator. You can ask Mr. Fortney."

Jason and Edward lay across Jason's bed, listening to KIDNEWS at 4:55. "A fast-breaking story just in from Shaw Park Lake," they heard Janice Conroy say. "An alligator was spotted on the lakeshore and in the water. The alligator is armed and dangerous. Armed with a mouthful of sharp teeth and a hearty appetite. And dangerous to the birds and fish and other wildlife who live at the lake. Remember, you heard it here first, from me, Janice Conroy, for KIDNEWS!"

Jason switched off the radio.

"See?" said Edward, "I told you."

"Told me what?" asked Jason.

"I told you I saw an alligator. And now you know it's true, because Janice Conroy said so on the radio," replied Edward.

"Janice Conroy said it on the radio because you told Marlene and Marilyn," said Jason.

"Do you think Janice would tell something on KIDNEWS that wasn't true?" said Edward.

"Of course not," Jason said. "I mean, not if she knew it wasn't true."

"Well, if she said it on the radio, and she wouldn't if it wasn't true, then you know it's true," Edward reasoned.

Jason groaned and rolled over onto his back. He stared in silent frustration at the model airplanes he'd made and hung up on wires from the ceiling of his bedroom.

Edward went to see what sort of snacks his mother had brought home from the market and to tell her what Janice Conroy had reported on KIDNEWS.

But Mrs. Fraser had been listening to the radio in the kitchen. "Guess what?" she said when Edward came in. "A bunch of people think they've seen an alligator over at Shaw Park Lake. They're saying it's five feet long, and hungry. Janice just took some calls about it on KIDNEWS."

"Janice said the alligator was five feet long?" asked Edward.

"No, it was someone who called in," his mother answered.

35

"How long is five feet?" Edward wanted to know.

"Well," said Mrs. Fraser, "that's about as long as Jason is."

Edward shook his head. "That's not right," he said.

"Yes, it is," his mother replied. "Jason was five feet tall last time he got measured."

"I don't mean Jason," said Edward. "I mean the alligator. It was nowhere near as long as Jason."

"Mmm," remarked Mrs. Fraser, taking food out of the grocery bags. "How long was it?"

Edward held his hands apart. "About this long," he answered.

"About three feet?" his mother asked.

Edward pushed his hands closer together. "More like this," he said.

"Mmm," she said again, "more like a foot and a half?"

"Yeah," said Edward, "just about."

"Must be a baby alligator, then," said Mrs. Fraser.

"Yes, it is," Edward agreed. "It is a baby. It's brown, and it has yellow stripes. Mr. Fortney and the encyclopedia both said that's the way baby alligators look."

"Edward," asked Mrs. Fraser, turning to face her son. "Just exactly what are we talking about?"

"The baby alligator I saw in Shaw Park Lake," said Edward.

"The baby alligator *you* saw?" she asked.

"In Shaw Park Lake," he said.

"I thought you were joking!" said Mrs. Fraser.

"Why would I joke about seeing an alligator?" Edward wanted to know.

"Well, I thought you meant crocodile. I thought you were pretending something about *Peter Pan*."

Edward could see his mother was confused. "Even if you thought I was joking, do you think Janice would joke on the radio?"

"No," his mother said. "I just—I didn't—"

"I wonder who would have called in and said it was five feet long?" said Edward.

"It sounded to me like Marilyn Conroy. Or Marlene."

"But they didn't see the alligator," Edward said. "They were hiding. I'm the one who saw it. They didn't know anything about it until I told them."

"Well, the caller said she saw it. She said it was five feet long and that it was gobbling up baby ducks."

"Did they say it went tick-tick-tick-tick?" asked Edward mischievously.

His mother thought. She shook her head, and

light bounced off the sparkly rhinestones that deco-
rated her black cat's-eye glasses. "I don't remember," she said. "Maybe they did. Did the alligator
you saw go tick-tick?"

"A joke, Mom," Edward said.

"I know that," his mother said.


Later, Mr. Fraser came home from work and burst
excitedly into the house. "Guess what?" he asked
his family.

"Ummm," said Edward.

"Hmmm?" said Mrs. Fraser.

"There's an alligator in Shaw Park Lake," said
Jason.

Mr. Fraser was impressed. "Good guess, Jason!"
he said.

# Animal Rights

Word traveled fast. It wasn't every day an alligator was spotted in Shaw Park Lake. The story was picked up from KIDNEWS by other programs and featured on the TV evening news.

"An alligator has been seen swimming in Shaw Park Lake," the newswoman said, looking serious.

"The zoo has been contacted, and a zookeeper and a zoo veterinarian plan to be at the lake tomorrow morning," the newsman added.

"Police and firefighters all have been alerted," continued the newswoman. "Rangers from the Park Service are already at the scene."

"And also at Shaw Park Lake, our own Brad

O'Brien is standing by. What's happening out there right now, Brad?"

Brad O'Brien appeared on the screen. He was standing on the shore of Shaw Park Lake, wearing a windbreaker with the collar turned up and holding a microphone. Two gangly park rangers stood next to him.

The reporter spoke into his microphone and looked directly into the camera. His image, with part of Shaw Park Lake behind him, filled the screen. "Brad O'Brien here, reporting live from Shaw Park Lake," he said. "And with me tonight at this usually peaceful neighborhood park are the two rangers in charge of open spaces and wildlife." He turned to one of the rangers and stuck the microphone in the man's face. "How big would you say this 'gator is, Ranger?"

"Couldn't say," the ranger mumbled.

Brad O'Brien quickly put the mike in front of the other ranger. "Just how big do these critters get?" he asked.

The second ranger took off his cap and thoughtfully scratched his head. "They can get right up there," he drawled. "Maybe eight, ten, even twelve feet long."

The newsman took back the mike and frowned.

40

"There you have it, folks," he said, in a serious, newsman-on-the-scene voice. "An unusual and possibly dangerous story is unfolding here in this quiet park, where children play and senior citizens stroll, but where the safety they take for granted has been shattered by the appearance of a dangerous reptile, possibly twelve feet long, which, for now, roams free and lurks somewhere beneath these seemingly quiet waters.

"How did it get here? How can it be safely captured and removed? These are the questions. So far, no one has the answers.

"Back to you in the studio, Blair and Sylvia!"

"Thanks, Brad," said the newswoman. "Well," she said, smiling and turning to the newsman, "seems to be quite an interesting story unfolding out there."

"You bet," the newsman agreed. Then he looked into the camera and addressed the people watching him on their TV screens. "Anyone who knows anything more about the reptilian invader of Shaw Park Lake is urged to call this number." A phone number appeared at the bottom of the screen. "Meanwhile, stay tuned to this channel for updates on the developing situation."

Just then the Frasers heard a helicopter flying

over their house. Edward put his hands over his ears. Jason and Mr. Fraser hurried to a window to see it. Mrs. Fraser picked up the remote and switched off the TV. She stared thoughtfully at the empty screen.

As soon as the noisy helicopter passed, Mrs. Fraser turned to Edward. "Well!" she said.

"Wow!" he exclaimed. "I guess the baby alligator I saw at the lake brought his dad with him!"

"Mmm," said Mrs. Fraser. "Or maybe the baby's grown a whole lot since you saw it this afternoon."

"Can things grow that fast?" asked Edward.

"Sometimes they can," his mother said, "once they get on the news."

The next morning, Edward was up and dressed at the crack of dawn. He wanted to be the first one at Shaw Park Lake. He wanted to get another look at the alligator. He wanted to see how much it had grown.

He passed Jason's room on his way to the kitchen for a quick breakfast. Jason was rolled up in his blanket and not moving.

"Jason," Edward whispered, "are you awake?"

Jason didn't answer.

"Jason?" Edward whispered louder. He tiptoed

into the room and stood quietly next to his brother's bed. "Jason?" he said.

"Grmmm," Jason groaned, covering his head.

"Want to go with me to the park and see if we can find the alligator?" asked Edward, putting his hand on Jason's shoulder and shaking just a little. "Do you?"

"Grmmmmmmm," Jason groaned again, rolling to the other side of his bed.

"Jason," Edward said, "if we don't hurry, everybody else will get there before we do."

Jason rolled over onto his back, pulled the blanket away from his face, squinted at the clock on his nightstand, and glared sleepily at Edward. "Do you know what time it is?"

Edward leaned over and looked at the clock. "Time to get up," he cracked.

It was almost 7 a.m. Edward had planned to be at the park by now.

Jason lay perfectly still and looked at his brother. Finally he said, "Edward, is this a school day?"

"Jason, you know it isn't. It's spring vacation."

"That's right," Jason said. "Now. Do we have any place we have to be this morning? Do we have a doctor's appointment? Do we have to go to the dentist? Is there an early baseball game?"

Edward giggled. "No," he said. "Nobody plays baseball at seven o'clock in the morning."

"That's right, Edward," Jason repeated.

"So?" asked Edward, waiting for Jason to get to the point.

"So—get out of my room and leave me alone. I'm sleeping." Jason closed his eyes and rolled over.

"Jason," Edward said cheerfully, "you're not sleeping. You're wide awake. You're talking to me."

"Edward, listen carefully," said Jason, his voice muffled by the blanket, which he'd pulled up over his head. "I'm sleeping. And I'm giving you three seconds to get out of my room. One . . . two . . ."

Edward sprang for the door and raced to the kitchen, where his father, dressed for work, was reading the newspaper and drinking a glass of orange juice.

"You're an early bird this morning," Mr. Fraser said, putting his juice glass into the sink and heading for the door. "And the early bird gets the worm!"

Was getting the worm a good thing or a bad thing, Edward wondered.

Edward got a high-energy-protein-apricot-oat bar out of the pantry. His mother bought the bars at a health-food store. They were very expensive, she

said, and they tasted like straw, but they were supposed to be as nutritious as a whole meal. And they were a lot easier to carry around. Edward would have preferred a banana. But the only ones they had were still too green to eat. He stuffed the oat bar into his pants pocket.

Then he got a pencil and a pad of paper out of the drawer where his mother kept rubber bands and pieces of string that were too short to use but too long to throw away.

"Mom, I am at the park," he wrote. "Love, Edward Fraser."

Edward fastened his helmet and hopped onto his bike. He rode quickly through the quiet streets, still hoping he'd be the first person at the lake. But when he got there, he saw he'd never had a chance. Parked right on the soccer field was a mobile TV van. A TV camera crew and some reporters stood next to it, chatting and drinking coffee out of Styrofoam cups.

The shy rangers the Frasers had seen on the news the night before were there, too, down near the water, holding what looked like butterfly nets. With the rangers were two women dressed in zookeeper's uniforms. And standing by himself,

46

scanning the lake through his binoculars, was Mr. Fortney.

Seven-thirty in the morning, and the place was mobbed!

Edward began walking around the lake. He peered into the water near the shore and farther out. He watched the reeds for any sign of something moving among them. He counted the turtles and ducks, the swans and the goose. He wanted to know how many there were to begin with, so he'd know if any more of them disappeared.

Edward practiced his Indian-tracking-a-wild-animal walk. He passed Mr. Fortney so quietly the teacher didn't notice him.

All around the lake Edward went. He went slowly and carefully, listening and looking. But he didn't see one thing out of the ordinary. And he didn't see any sign of an alligator, large *or* small.

By the time Edward got back to his starting place near the park entrance, more people had arrived.

The Conroys were there. Janice Conroy was talking to the rangers and the zoo people. She was taking notes. She wore a big badge pinned to her shirt that said "KIDNEWS."

Marlene and Marilyn Conroy were there, also.

They had already set up two tables. On one, they had propped a hand-lettered sign that said, "Gatorade, 25 cents."

Marlene sat behind this table on a folding chair and got ready to sell people small paper cups half-full of Gatorade, which she poured out of a big, economy-sized jug she kept next to her on the ground.

On the second table, the Conroys had put up a sign showing something that looked sort of like an alligator eating something that looked sort of like a chicken. "Duck decoys!" the sign advertised. "Fool the alligator! Protect the real ducks!"

Mr. Conroy, the girls' father, was nearby, chatting with Officer Mendez, who stood next to her bicycle. "My girls are nothing if not enterprising," bragged Mr. Conroy. Officer Mendez nodded in agreement. "And they always like to have their ducks lined up! Ha-ha!" he joked.

Officer Mendez looked puzzled.

"You know," Mr. Conroy explained, "ducks in a row? Lined up? Means they like to know what's happening next and decide ahead of time what to do about it. They're organized. And persuasive. Why, they got me to take them over to the mall last night to buy those bath-toy ducks when I was about too pooped to pop! They're real go-getters."

"Oh, yes," said the officer, smiling.

"Sure wish I could stay and watch the circus," said Mr. Conroy, "but I'm late for work already. I'll have to hear about it on KIDNEWS. That's my daughter Janice's radio show," he boasted, heading for his car. Officer Mendez nodded and waved goodbye to Mr. Conroy. Then she pushed off and mounted her bike.

Edward decided to walk around the lake again. He would circle it until he saw the alligator.

Edward started walking. He studied every shadow. He noticed every ripple. His eyes felt keen. In the green and golden morning light, he felt he could see things almost as clearly as he could if he were looking through Mr. Fortney's binoculars. Slow and measured step-by-step, he circled the lake again.

When he got back to the starting place, even more people had come. An opened-up ironing board now stood near the Conroys' tables. A bedsheet was hung over the ironing board, and painted in red letters on the bedsheet were the words "Animal Rights."

A big glass jar with a dollar bill inside it stood on the ironing board. The label on the jar said, " 'Gator Aid." A man and a woman stood behind the ironing board, looking as if they were behind a counter in a store. They both had on big sun hats, and they both looked worried.

By noon, Edward had lost count of how many times he'd gone around the lake. And he didn't even try to count all the people who were crowding into the park. Why, it was full of people, and almost all of them were hanging around the TV van.

Edward was sure the alligator would be too shy to show itself to such a mob. He thought of asking Mr. Fortney if he could look through his binoculars again. But he decided against it. He would go back and keep watch on the other side of the lake, where it was quiet.

Edward sat down by himself and kept his eyes glued to the water. Just as he was starting to feel bored to death and to wonder if anything interesting was happening over where all the people were, his friends Jeffrey Sanders and Denny Marks came whooping along the pathway, shooting suction-cup darts at each other. When they saw Edward, they came over and sat down, too.

"What are you doing?" Jeffrey wanted to know.

"Watching for the alligator," Edward answered.

"Do you think it's still here?" Denny asked.

Edward nodded. "Where else could it be?"

Denny shrugged. "It could be where it was before the Conroys saw it yesterday," he answered. "It could have gone back."

Edward felt put-out. "The Conroys didn't see an alligator yesterday," he said.

"Sure they did," said Jeffrey. "It was on the news."

"That doesn't matter," insisted Edward. "News reporters say anything anyone tells them."

"No, they don't," argued Denny. "They have to check it out before they can say it."

"That's true, Edward," said Jeffrey.

"I know they're supposed to check it out," said Edward, "but I don't think they did this time. Because I was here yesterday. And I know for a fact the Conroys did *not* see an alligator."

"You mean nobody has actually seen an alligator in this lake?" asked Denny.

"I didn't say that," said Edward. "I just said it wasn't the Conroys."

"Who saw it, then?"

"Me. I saw it."

"Oh, sure."

"I did. I saw it," Edward insisted. "I told the Conroys about it, and they took the credit. But I'm the one who saw the alligator."

"Cross your heart?"

Edward nodded and with his finger drew a big X across his chest.

"Was it twelve feet long?"

"No."

"Ten?"

"Nope."

"Eight?"

"It was this big," Edward said, holding his hands less than two feet apart.

"Oh, right, Edward," Denny said. "I'm sure some fierce alligator is just that big." He crossed his eyes at Edward.

"It's a baby," Edward said.

"A baby?" Denny exclaimed. "Are you telling us that all this fuss is over a baby just that long?" He put his hands about three inches apart.

"That long," Edward corrected, showing him again how long the baby alligator was.

Jeffrey was still thinking about the Conroys. "It doesn't make any difference who saw it yesterday," he reasoned. "Somebody has to see it today. And then they have to figure out how to catch it and get it to the zoo without hurting it."

"What if they hurt it while they're trying to catch it?" Denny wanted to know.

"That would be wrong," said Jeffrey.

"I mean, what if they hurt it by accident," said Denny.

"It would still be wrong. They have to figure out how to catch it without hurting it."

"What if the alligator hurts them? Is that wrong, too?"

"You don't have to look out for people," said Edward. "People can take care of themselves."

"You must be kidding!" said Denny. "You don't have to look out for people who are catching alligators? Alligators, with sharp teeth and big claws and slashing tails? You've got to be kidding!"

Just then Edward saw the alligator. It was out on the island, creeping through reeds, heading for the water.

Edward sat stiffly and kept perfectly still. "Shhh," he warned, barely moving his mouth, "there it is!"

"Where?" whispered Jeffrey.

"Where?" asked Denny.

Edward pointed. But by the time the other boys looked, the baby alligator had slipped into the water and disappeared.

Denny jumped to his feet. "Alligator!" he hollered. "Alligator!"

The rangers and the zookeeper and reporters came hurrying around the lake.

They all spoke at once. "Who saw it? Where? What was it doing? Was it hurt? How long was it? What color was it? Where did it go?"

Jeffrey and Edward stood up. "He saw it," Jeffrey said, pointing at Edward.

"I almost saw it!" said Denny.

"You the only one who saw it?" a reporter asked Edward. Edward nodded.

"And he's the only one who saw it yesterday, too," said Jeffrey helpfully. "And it's a tiny baby alligator only about so big." He held his hands about twelve inches apart.

"Kids just want some attention," the cameraman decided, turning away.

"That isn't true!" said Edward. "It went into the water right over there. And it was the same alligator I saw yesterday. It was a baby, and it was brown with yellow stripes. And—and it was smiling!"

"Whoa, *smiling*!" said one of the rangers. "Kid's got one active imagination."

Everyone straggled away. Jeffrey, Denny, and Edward followed.

"Did you really see it, Edward?" Jeffrey asked again.

"Yes, I did," Edward said. "I told you."

"I know," Jeffrey said. "But, well, you do have a big imagination, Edward. And you didn't say anything about smiling until the reporters came."

"I didn't know how to explain how it looked!" protested Edward. "I couldn't think of the way to say it till right then."

"Never mind," said Denny. "Who cares? Let's play cops-and-robbers."

"I can't," said Edward. "I don't have my gun."

"Go home and get it," suggested Jeffrey.

"That's okay," Edward said. "I don't feel like playing right now."

"Okay," said Denny, "see you later, then."

"Yeah, see you later, alligator!" cracked Jeffrey.

"After a while, crocodile," cracked Denny.

"Ha-ha. Very funny," said Edward to himself, as his two friends raced off.

Mr. Fortney was still on the lakeshore, stubbornly looking and looking through his binoculars.

Edward was disappointed that nobody else had seen the little alligator. He'd heard the cameraman say he was making it up to get attention, and that hurt his feelings. He went to stand by Mr. Fortney.

"Did you see the baby alligator yet, Mr. Fortney?" he asked.

"Not yet," the teacher answered. "I haven't even seen the big one everyone is making such a fuss about."

Edward was silent. "Do you think I have an active imagination?" he asked finally.

Mr. Fortney smiled as he looked through his binoculars. "You certainly do," he said.

Tears came into Edward's eyes. Even his teacher thought he was a liar. Without meaning to, he snuffled.

"Why, Edward," Mr. Fortney exclaimed, taking the binoculars away from his eyes and looking at Edward, "what in the world is the matter?"

"Everyone thinks I'm a liar," said Edward. "And I'm not." He remembered to cross his fingers behind his back before saying, "I never lie."

"I didn't say I thought you were a liar," said the teacher. "I said you have a good imagination. That was a compliment."

"It was?" said Edward.

"It was," Mr. Fortney assured him.

57

"Could I look through the binoculars?" Edward asked.

"Of course," answered Mr. Fortney. "Look as long as you like. Take your time."

Edward scanned the shore and the lake. The goose was scolding, but she kept her distance from the crowd. The swans were gliding along. They didn't seem worried. The turtles were lined up on their log. The yellow decoys that Marlene was selling were bobbing around all over the place. The real ducks and the grebes were paddling and circling, as usual. And there was the duck family. It was the same one Edward had seen the day before, the father duck, the mother duck, and the four ducklings.

Four?

Four!

# Pirates!

Edward felt as if he had something caught in his throat. "Mr. Fortney," he said, "look! Four ducklings!"

The teacher looked. "Cute little things," he murmured.

"But Mr. Fortney, there are only four of them."

"That's not unusual, Edward. Often a duck family will have only three or four ducklings. Only two, sometimes. It's nothing to worry about."

"But Mr. Fortney, remember yesterday?"

"Yes," Mr. Fortney said.

"There were five—uh—six yesterday."

"Five?" said Mr. Fortney.

"Six," said Edward.

"Yesterday there were five or six ducklings?" the teacher repeated.

"Yes," Edward answered.

"And now there are four?"

"Yes."

"And you're sure how many there were yesterday?"

"Yes!"

"How many?"

"Six!"

"Or five?"

"Well, yes," Edward admitted.

"Or maybe," the teacher coached, "maybe *four*?"

Edward looked down. He knew what answer his teacher wanted. "Maybe," he said. But his fingers were tightly crossed behind his back.

Edward was hungry. He pulled the apricot oat bar out of the pocket of his jeans. "Would you like some?" he said politely.

Mr. Fortney eyeballed the crushed bar. "No thanks," he said. Then he took a bologna sandwich wrapped in waxed paper out of his jacket pocket. "Would you like half a sandwich?" he asked.

Edward stuffed the oat bar back into his pants and took half of the bologna-and-mustard sandwich from Mr. Fortney. When they finished eating, Mr. Fortney bought two small cups of Gatorade from Marilyn, who was doing a brisk business.

"Fifty cents, please," said Marilyn, handing the half-full cups to the teacher.

"Highway robbery," said Mr. Fortney pleasantly, taking them from her and giving one to Edward.

Marilyn smiled innocently. "Thank you, Mr. Fortney," she said.

"You're welcome, Marilyn."

"Highway robbery?" asked Edward.

"Just an expression," said Mr. Fortney.

"An expression?"

"A saying," explained the teacher.

"A saying?"

"A shortcut."

"A shortcut?" asked Edward, thinking of the shortcut through the vacant lot that he and Jason took when they walked to Jason's baseball practice.

"It means charging too much for what you're selling," said Mr. Fortney.

"Oh, the Conroys always do that," Edward explained. He repeated what he'd heard Mr. Conroy tell Officer Mendez. "The Conroys are enterprising."

"Yes," said Mr. Fortney, "and so were the highway robbers and pirates in the old days. Very enterprising."

Pirates! Edward had forgotten all about pirates. Now he looked around for Captain Hook, for Smee, for the rest of the kids who had been in the play. The fifth-graders were missing! Not one of them was at the park.

Probably they were all still home in bed, too tired from being in the play Sunday night to pay attention to the most exciting thing that had ever happened in the neighborhood.

Edward made up his mind then and there never to be in a play. It wouldn't be worth it, not if it made you that tired.

But he was wrong. Because here they came now, all the fifth-graders, including Jason, in their costumes, herded by Ms. Bascombe right up to the shore and right under the noses of the news reporters and the TV photographers, who had been standing around all morning waiting for something to report and something to film.

Up to that moment, the story seemed to be that there was no story. But when they saw the fifth-

graders in their costumes, the reporters and photographers perked up. If they couldn't get pictures
of an alligator, at least they could get pictures of
this.

The fifth-graders stood in two rows. Ms. Bascombe
stood in front, directing them. They recited the two
pirate chants from *Peter Pan*. The first one went:

> *"The splintry plank*
> *Set over the side*
> *Ye walk along it so,*
> *Till it go down*
> *And you go down*
> *To Davy Jones below,*
> *Ho! Ho!"*

The second one went:

> *"Yo ho, yo ho, the scratching cat,*
> *It's got nine tails, you know,*
> *And when it hits you on the back*
> *You beg to go below, ho! ho!*
> *To Davy Jones' locker below!"*

Edward thought they were finished. Those were
the only two chants he remembered from the play.

But the cameraman called out, "One more!" And Ms. Bascombe rounded up the students, who had started to wander off.

This time, they struggled through all the verses of "Puff the Magic Dragon," and when they finished, Janice and one other reporter interviewed Ms. Bascombe.

"It's in their blood!" the teacher cried, closing her blue-painted eyelids and putting her hand over her heart. "They're all going to be stars!"

"Why did you choose that particular song to sing down here by the lake today, ma'am?" the reporter asked.

"It's clear, isn't it?" said Ms. Bascombe, blinking her eyelids in a surprised way.

"Um, well, yes, but perhaps you should tell our audience," said the reporter. He motioned toward the camera.

"What is more like a dragon of old," she cried, as if she were speaking from a stage, "than the alligator of today? Or the crocodile, of course."

"So, your class was singing to the dragon," said Janice. "I mean, to the alligator."

"Serenading the poor lost creature," said Ms. Bascombe.

"And let me get this straight," the reporter interrupted. "These kids sang 'Puff the Magic Dragon' for this occasion because . . . ?"

"Because it is so suitable," said Ms. Bascombe, smiling sweetly.

"And because it's the song we've been learning to sing for Parents' Night," called out Arnie Pollack.

Ms. Bascombe took a deep breath and fake-smiled in Arnie's direction. "That, too, of course," she admitted.

"Did you think the song might bring the alligator out of hiding?" Janice asked.

"Mmmmm," Ms. Bascombe replied.

"Why don't you try it again?" said the reporter, motioning to the cameraman to come around in front of the embarrassed fifth-graders.

"A wonderful idea!" the teacher cried, as her students groaned. She clapped her hands. "Boys and girls!" she called. " 'Puff the Magic Dragon' one more time, if you please. Remember, you are the alligator's friends. You love him because he is magical." Her voice changed from sweetness to a tough, show-business tone. "Now—give it all you've got!"

The reluctant fifth-graders sang.

"Sweetly, sweetly," urged the teacher.

"There it is!" shouted Alexander Friedman. "Right over there!"

Everyone rushed to the water's edge. But by the time they got there the alligator was gone.

The Animal Rights people, the zookeeper, and the zoo veterinarian now spoke to the newsmen. Edward stood close by, so he could listen.

"This is inhumane treatment!" declared the Animal Rights man. "We can't allow this to continue!"

Edward guessed he hadn't liked the songs.

"How do you expect us to catch a wild animal with a circus going on?" demanded the zookeeper. "Someone has got to restore order in this park!"

Edward figured she hadn't liked the songs, either.

Like almost everyone else in the neighborhood, the Frasers watched all of it on the news that night. They saw Officer Mendez politely tell everyone they would have to go, unless they had an official reason for being in the park after dark.

As the people left, they saw her string yellow tape around the lakeshore, as if it were the scene of a crime.

Then there were shots of the fifth-grade chorus.

"Look, Dad," cried Edward. "There's Jason singing 'Puff the Magic Dragon.'"

"I am not singing," declared Jason.

"That's true," observed Mrs. Fraser. "Your mouth isn't moving at all."

"I bet he was humming," Edward teased.

"I was not humming," growled Jason.

"Shhh," Mr. Fraser said, "let's listen."

"Chaos at the lake," said the TV newsman.

"Only one alleged alligator sighting," said the newswoman.

"Unruly crowds," they continued. "Police control needed."

"And here's the latest report, just in from Alligator Central," said the newswoman. "The Animal Rights Society says they have hired Captain Jim-Bob Hooke, a professional alligator catcher from Opelousas, Louisiana, to come and help us catch our alligator.

"Contacted by this station, Captain Hooke assured us that he and his assistant would be here by noon tomorrow, prepared to spend the rest of the week helping to catch the Shaw Park Lake alligator.

"Captain Hooke said, and I quote, 'I've caught about a thousand alligators, and I never hurt a one of them. You people seem to be in trouble up there, and I'm proud to come 'n help you out.'

"That's Captain Jim-Bob Hooke, who . . ."

The newscasters kept talking, but Edward and Jason had stopped listening.

"*Captain Hook?*" asked Edward.

"Tick-tick-tick-tick!" replied Jason.

Then they both cracked up.

# Captain Hooke

The next day, just about everyone in the neighborhood who didn't have to be someplace else headed for Shaw Park Lake to watch for the alligator and wait for the arrival of Captain Jim-Bob Hooke, the licensed alligator-control agent from Louisiana.

There were teenagers riding on skateboards and babies riding in strollers. There were rollerbladers. There were determined-looking four- and five-year-olds wearing serious helmets and riding tiny two-wheelers with training wheels. More than a few people brought their laptop computers, so they could work while they waited. Some of the older neighbors brought lawn chairs to sit on. And Mrs. Porter came in her motorized wheelchair.

The zookeeper passed out flyers describing the habits of alligators and warning people to be careful to keep pets, small children, hands, and feet out of the water. The Animal Rights people and Marlene and Marilyn Conroy were back at their posts, and the TV van was parked in its usual place, with the TV camera people and the reporters lounging nearby.

Janice Conroy worked the crowd, asking questions and writing down the answers people gave her in her reporter's notebook. Jason and some of the other fifth-graders stood together on the far side of the lake, as far away from the TV cameras as they could get. Mrs. Fraser stood next to Mr. Fortney, peering through her binoculars every bit as intently as he peered through his. And Edward, who had come prepared, armed with his dart gun, was playing cops-and-robbers with his friends.

The hours passed. The yellow tape fell to the ground, and nobody bothered to put it up again. Finally, as the afternoon wore on, people began to get their things together and leave the park. "No alligator and no alligator catcher," they grumbled, as they squeezed their trash into the overflowing garbage cans.

A cool breeze came up, and clouds drifted in front of the sun. Edward went to stand next to his mother and Mr. Fortney, two determined people still scanning the lake through their binoculars.

"See anything?" Edward asked.

"Everything but," his mother answered.

"Everything but what?" Edward asked.

"Everything but the alligator."

"Mr. Fortney?" asked Edward.

"Me too," the teacher said. "Everything but."

"Can I look?" asked Edward.

"May I," said Mrs. Fraser and Mr. Fortney at the same time.

"Sure you may," cracked Edward, "they're your binoculars!"

"Very funny," said Mrs. Fraser, who was tired of that old joke. She handed her binoculars to Edward.

Edward adjusted them and slowly looked all around the lake. No sign of the alligator. Just the grebes swimming in circles and the duck family, over there by the reeds—the father duck, the mother duck, and the three ducklings.

Three?

Three!

Edward handed back his mother's binoculars. "The alligator's definitely still here," he told her sadly.

"How do you know?" she asked.

"Did you see it?" Mr. Fortney wanted to know.

"Nope," Edward answered.

"Then how can you be sure it's still here?" asked Mrs. Fraser, readjusting the binoculars for her eyes.

Edward shrugged. "I can tell," he said.

Just then they heard excited voices coming from the direction of the park entrance. Captain Jim-Bob Hooke had finally arrived!

The Louisiana alligator expert was a husky man with a trim gray beard. He had on work boots and blue jeans and a belt with a big shiny brass buckle made in the shape of a sharp-toothed, open-jawed, tail-thrashing alligator.

At the trapper's side stood a serious-looking eleven-year-old girl, the trapper's granddaughter, Earline Hooke. She was wearing boots and blue jeans and a belt with a big shiny brass alligator buckle, just like his.

Captain Hooke seemed surprised to see so much going on in the park. He seemed confused when the reporters peppered him with questions and the TV camera people started taping.

Every time someone threw a question at him, he'd look in their direction, and while he was considering the question and thinking about his answer, someone else would call out another question and he'd look in that direction. The television cameras were pointed at him and running, and everyone who was still in the park was crowded around as close as they could get.

Jim-Bob Hooke was getting more and more flustered.

But his granddaughter, Earline, wasn't at all flustered. She just stood still, with her pale eyes scrunched and her hands stuck into the front pockets of her jeans. She didn't look at anyone who asked Captain Hooke a question. She kept her eyes on the lake.

"Look there, Granddaddy," she said quietly, tugging at the trapper's sleeve to get his attention. "Looky. There it is."

"There what is, honey?" her grandfather asked, putting his hand behind one ear to show her he couldn't hear what she was saying.

Earline spoke up. "There's the 'gator," she said, "right over there in the reeds."

Almost everyone within earshot rushed to the lakeshore. Mr. Fortney and Mrs. Fraser joined the others. But Edward, wide-eyed, stayed right where he was. He'd already seen the alligator. But he'd never in his life seen anything as beautiful as those alligator belt buckles.

"Earline, honey," said Jim-Bob Hooke, "you really see the crittur?"

Earline shook her head yes. "It was right over there," she said, pointing. "It was swimmin' in the reeds with its big old bulgy eyes stickin' out above the water. It looked more like a bullfrog than a 'gator, Granddaddy."

"That small?" said Jim-Bob.

"Nothin' to it, Granddaddy," she said, putting her hands about three feet apart. "Not a speck bigger 'n this."

She *did* see it, thought Edward.

But nobody else did. Soon the onlookers and the reporters straggled back to where Captain Hooke and Earline were standing.

Now Earline took command. "My granddaddy's suddenly got him a sore throat," she announced.

"And he asked me to remind you this here's *your* alligator. We're only here to help."

"How do you plan to hunt the alligator?" asked a reporter.

"Hunt!" cried the Animal Rights lady.

"Um, how do you plan to capture the alligator?" asked another.

"Capture!" cried the Animal Rights man.

"My granddaddy plans to—rescue—the baby alligator tonight," said Earline. "He'll use this." She picked up a seven-foot-long fishing pole from the baggage on the ground at Captain Hooke's feet. "And this." She showed the crowd some twenty-pound fishing line. "And this." She displayed a roll of electrical tape. "And this." She gestured toward a dog kennel with a door in front. "And this." She held up a special, three-pronged hook.

"What's he going to do with all that stuff?"

"He's goin' to attach the hook to the line and the line to the fishin' pole," Earline explained. "Then he's goin' to cast it out to where he sees the 'gator. And then he's goin' to reel the crittur in, sit on him, tape his jaws shut, and shove him into the carryin' box."

"That hook will hurt it!" objected the Animal Rights lady.

"No, ma'am," Earline answered politely. "Alligator skin is tough as anything. The 'gator won't feel this hook any more'n you would if it snagged your shirt."

Janice Conroy spoke up. "When does your grandfather plan to get to work?"

"Later tonight," Earline told her. "We'll come back when y'all's park is quiet. We'll shine this all around"—she picked up a large flashlight—"until we see that 'gator's eyes shinin' back at us. And then Granddaddy'll snare—I mean rescue—the 'gator."

"What makes you so sure it'll come out so you can shine the light in its eyes?" Janice persisted.

"Oh, Granddaddy intends to call it," said Earline. "He'll do his alligator call, and it'll come out to see where the other 'gator is.

"Granddaddy's one of the champion alligator—um, rescuers—in the state of Louisiana. He's rescued prob'ly a thousand 'gators," she added. "And he's won first prize in the 'gator-callin' competition at the state fair for ten years in a row."

Jim-Bob Hooke flushed proudly and looked shy.

"Can you let us hear that alligator call, Mr. Hooke?"

The man looked at his granddaughter. She nod-

ded. "But not too loud, Granddaddy," she warned. "We don't want the 'gator to think we're teasin' it."

Jim-Bob Hooke motioned for the reporters and camera people to step up close. And then he demonstrated his alligator call. "Hunh," he cooed. "Hunh, hunh."

No one there had ever heard a sound quite like it. "Authentic," said one of the reporters to another. "This guy knows his business," decided a third.

"Hunh," Edward said softly to himself, imitating Captain Hooke's alligator imitation. "Hunh, hunh."

Then Trapper Jim-Bob Hooke and his granddaughter Earline and all their stuff were whisked away by the representative from the Animal Rights Society who'd brought them from the airport.

"Time to go," Mrs. Fraser said, putting her hand on Edward's shoulder.

"Hunh," said Edward. "I mean, now?"

"Now," his mother replied.

"But Mom, they're coming back to catch the alligator."

"Catch?" Mrs. Fraser joked.

"I mean rescue," said Edward. "They are going to rescue it, aren't they?"

"Actually they are, Edward," said Mr. Fortney,

who was walking with them. "You see, alligators need to live in warm climates. They need to swim in warm water and lie around in the sunshine. If they can't do that, they get chilled and catch colds. You'd have one sick alligator on your hands if you left it in a cool place like this for very long."

Mr. Fortney waved goodbye and went to his car.

Edward and Mrs. Fraser walked home.

A cool wind stirred the branches of the trees. Edward thought about the baby alligator in the cold water. He was glad Captain Hooke had come. But he wondered why a warm place like Louisiana needed alligators rescued all the time.

"How come so many alligators need rescuing?" he asked his mother. She looked inquiringly at him.

"Earline said her granddad had rescued thousands of alligators. How come so many alligators need rescuing in a warm place like Louisiana?"

"I think 'rescue' is a nice way of saying catch," Mrs. Fraser answered. "In the newspaper it said Captain Hooke was a 'nuisance-alligator control agent, registered and licensed in Louisiana.' "

"What's a nuisance?" asked Edward.

Jason had caught up and was walking with them.

"A nuisance is an alligator that asks questions all the time," he said, trying to step on Edward's foot.

"Oh, sure," said Edward, trying to step on Jason's foot.

Edward wanted to go back to the park after dinner to watch the alligator catcher work. But his mother didn't have time. She had to prepare for the class in small-appliance repair she was teaching at the recreation center. And his father said he was tired from work and would just as soon watch it all on TV. "They're broadcasting the whole thing live," he told Edward. "We'll be able to see whatever happens. And we'll have front-row seats and all the comforts of home."

"Hunh," said Edward.

"Huh?" asked Mr. Fraser.

"Well, what about Jason?" Edward asked.

"What about Jason?" said Jason.

"Can I—may I go to the park if Jason comes with me?"

"Jason can't come with you," Jason said.

"Why not?" asked Edward.

"Because Jason has to practice," Jason answered.

"Practice what?" asked Mr. Fraser.

"Air-guitar," Mrs. Fraser told him.

"That's funny," said Mr. Fraser. "I used to play air-guitar, and I never needed to practice."

After supper, Mrs. Fraser went to work at her computer. Jason went to his room. Mr. Fraser sat down on the couch in the family room, put his feet up on one end of the coffee table, turned on the TV, and fell asleep. Edward got his pens and scissors and some paper and shirt cardboards. He kneeled on the floor and used the free end of the coffee table to draw on.

He drew a small alligator. Then he drew two big ones. All his alligators were ferocious, with open mouths that seemed to be smiling in a scary, alligator way, and rows of sharp teeth. They had strong, slashing tails. They looked like the alligator belt buckles Jim-Bob Hooke and his granddaughter wore.

Carefully, Edward colored the alligators and cut them out. He pasted the small one onto a piece of shirt cardboard. He cut it out again and taped it to the front of his belt. Then, holding the other two in his hand, he crept down the hallway to Jason's room.

Jason's door was partly open. Edward slid along the wall until he could peek in without being seen.

He tried to make up his mind whether to say Tick-tick-tick or Hunh-hunh-hunh. Which one would get Jason interested in having a fight with the paper alligators?

While he was trying to make up his mind, he heard Jason say, "Forget it!" and hang up the phone. Then he heard Jason say, "Girls!"

Edward forgot about the paper-alligator fight. He scooted into Jason's room. "What about girls?" he asked.

"What are you doing in here?" Jason replied.

"Nothing," said Edward. "What are you doing?"

"Nothing," admitted Jason.

"Want to play?"

"Play what?"

Edward showed Jason the alligators he'd made. "Alligator fight?"

"Your alligators will get wrecked if we do that," Jason pointed out.

"I don't care," said Edward. "I can make more." Jason shrugged. "Here," said Edward, handing Jason an alligator.

Jason took the alligator, made a fierce noise, and attacked. The two alligators wrestled until they were both badly torn.

"Give?" asked Jason's alligator.

"No!" cried Edward's alligator.

They fought some more, until they were both ruined. Jason crumpled his up and tossed it in the general direction of the wastebasket.

"Missed," Edward announced. He crumpled his alligator and, concentrating and eyeing the wastebasket, tossed it.

"Missed," said Jason.

Edward crawled over to the wastebasket and got both crumpled pieces of paper. He gave one to Jason. "Let's try again," he said. "Loser has to answer the winner's question."

Jason rolled his eyes and flipped the paper at the wastebasket. It bounced off the rim and onto the floor.

"Missed, Jas," said Edward happily, squinting at the wastebasket and aiming.

"Duh," said Jason.

Edward aimed and aimed. Jason watched. Finally, Edward said, "Here goes!" Jason roared a fierce alligator roar just as Edward started to throw. Edward missed by a mile.

"Jason!" Edward objected.

"Edward!" Jason mimicked.

"If I won, I was going to ask you what *about* girls?" said Edward.

"And if I won, I was going to ask you why you're such a weirdo," said Jason.

Mr. Fraser knocked loudly on Jason's open door. "Program's on," he announced.

The three of them hurried to the family room. Mrs. Fraser was already there, sitting on the couch with her eyes glued to the TV set and a huge bowl of popcorn on her lap. Jason and Edward sat on either side of her. They each took a handful of popcorn. Mr. Fraser reached over the back of the couch and helped himself to some.

"Why don't you turn off the sound," Mrs. Fraser suggested. "Then we can watch without having to listen to all that talk."

"Good idea," said Mr. Fraser, silencing the TV with the remote.

There was Jim-Bob Hooke and his granddaughter being driven up to the entrance of the park. "That's Captain *Hooke*," said Edward, giggling.

"Tick-tick," added Jason.

"Shhh," said Mr. Fraser and Mrs. Fraser.

The picture on the silent screen showed the alligator trapper and his granddaughter getting out of a car and walking into the park, accompanied by the rangers, the zookeeper, and the zoo veterinarian. It showed the Animal Rights table still set up,

and the Animal Rights people still on duty, now wearing warm knitted caps instead of sun hats. The bedsheet with "Animal Rights" written on it fluttered in the evening breeze.

Earline carried the dog kennel. Captain Hooke had the rest of his gear. Over one shoulder he carried the seven-foot-long fishing pole, strung with the twenty-pound line and armed with the three-pronged alligator hook. The tape he would need to tape the alligator's snapping jaws together was stuffed into his shirt pocket. In his other hand he carried a large flashlight.

"He's going to shine that light all around until it hits the alligator's eyes. When he sees them shining back at him, he'll strike," Mrs. Fraser explained to Mr. Fraser.

Just then another camera must have swung into action, because the image on the screen changed. Now the Frasers could see only a close-up of the trapper's concentrating face. And now they couldn't see anything. Something had happened, and the picture was slanted and blurry.

Mr. Fraser turned on the sound. They heard the announcer's excited voice, "Blinded by the light on one of our TV cameras coming in for a close shot, Captain Hooke stumbled and . . ." Here the voice broke off, and the Frasers heard the sound of water spraying and saw that all the automatic sprinklers in the park had come on!

Then they heard the news announcer's excited voice again. "Just as Jim-Bob Hooke, the Louisiana alligator expert, got to his feet after being accidentally blinded by the light on one of our cameras and tripping over the Animal Rights ironing board, still off-balance from his first fall, he was surprised by the park sprinklers, set on a timer to go off automatically, and he fell again. Is he hurt?"

The camera photographing the TV newsman bobbed, and again the image on the screen was a blur. Another camera took over and focused on the pandemonium, and the Frasers and everyone else watching finally could see what was going on. There was Trapper Hooke, sitting on the ground, looking stunned. The Animal Rights ironing board lay turned over at his side, and the sheet with "Animal Rights" written on it was draped over his chest.

Earline and the zookeeper were trying to help the alligator catcher up. The park rangers were standing over him, looking confused. And the whole bunch of them were getting completely soaked by the automatic sprinklers.

From off-camera came the sound of a siren and

the rapid voice of the TV reporter. "Trapper Jim-Bob Hooke, down for the second time, may be hurt. He is—yes, he is hurt. It's his arm. No, it's his wrist. Looks like it may be both his wrists! The alligator trapper is down and out, folks, undone not by his reptilian foe but by the light shining into his eyes from a TV camera; not by wrestling with an alligator but by tangling with the Animal Rights sheet; not by slipping in the water at the edge of the lake as he tried to reel in the critter, but by sliding on the wet grass. Looks like Jim-Bob Hooke is down for the count."

The camera pulled away from the trapper and panned around the lakeshore, as if trying to give the viewers one shot of the gleaming eyes of the alligator. But all it managed to show was the shadowy park at night.

"Alligator 1, alligator catcher 0," said Jason.

"To be continued," said Mrs. Fraser.

"Maybe not," said Mr. Fraser. "The star player on our team may be out of the game." He stood up and stretched. "Anyone want something to drink?" he asked.

"Me," said Jason, getting up to go into the kitchen with his father.

"I do," said Mrs. Fraser, getting up, too.

"What about you, Edward?" asked Mrs. Fraser. "Want a cold drink?"

Edward didn't answer. He kept his eyes glued on the shadowy screen. He watched the fuzzy images of the park at night as the camera took a long, lazy look around.

Mrs. Fraser waited a moment. Then she followed Mr. Fraser and Jason into the kitchen.

Edward sat, transfixed, in front of the screen. "Hunh," he said softly to himself. And then he caught his breath, for there before him on the television screen, sliding behind trees on the far side of the lake, was a shadow—a shadow that looked just like a dog. "Rooter!" cried Edward. But the camera had moved on, and he couldn't be sure.

Edward started to rush into the kitchen to tell his family. Then he stopped himself. He knew Jason would say something about his imagination. And he was tired of being accused of having a good imagination. He decided he wouldn't say anything to anyone until he could come up with the proof and his imagination didn't have any way of getting involved.

The camera turned its eye back to the lakeshore and moved around, as if still looking for an alligator.

And Edward saw that shadow again, now stiffly limping away from the lake.

"Jason! Mom! Dad!" he called. "Here's Rooter! I found Rooter!"

Jason and Mr. and Mrs. Fraser hurried back into the family room. Jason rushed to the window.

"Where?" they all asked Edward. "Where's Rooter?"

Edward got up and went over to the television set. He put his finger just exactly where he'd seen the shadow. "He was right there."

"There?" Mr. Fraser asked.

"Where?" Mrs. Fraser wanted to know.

"Edward," Jason said, "what are you talking about?"

"About Rooter," Edward answered.

"I know that, Edward," Jason replied. "But I thought you said you found him."

"I did find him!"

"Then where is he?"

"He's right here, right where my finger is. I mean, he *was* right where my finger is."

"They showed Rooter on television?" asked Mr. Fraser.

"They were showing the lake," Edward explained, "and I saw him over in the bushes on the other side. And then I saw him again, right here."

"You saw Rooter?" Mrs. Fraser asked. "Were they shining lights over there?"

Edward hesitated. "No," he said.

"Then how could you see anything that was over there?" asked Jason.

"I could, Jason. I could see a lot. I could see bushes and trees and shadows. And one of the shadows was limping."

"Sure it was," Jason said. "And one of the other shadows was playing hackey-sack."

"Really?" said Edward. "I didn't see that one."

"No, not really," Jason said, exasperated. "Of course not."

"Then why did you say it was?"

"Jason was trying—in a not particularly nice way—to say that he doesn't believe you saw Rooter," said Mrs. Fraser, frowning at Jason.

"Why would I lie about something like that?" Edward wanted to know.

"I didn't mean you were lying," Jason replied, "about that. I just meant that, well, that your imagination was working overtime again. Why don't you give it a rest?"

"Give it a rest? Give it a rest?" cried Edward. "Why doesn't *it* give *me* a rest for a change?"

"Too much TV, it seems to me," said Mr. Fraser, turning off the set.

"Too much excitement for one day," agreed Mrs. Fraser.

"Too much imagination for one kid," said Jason.

Edward didn't have anything to say. He knew what he'd seen. And he planned to be at the park first thing in the morning, before even the TV people were there, to look for Rooter.

# Imagination

Edward stole into the park early the next morning, before the camera crew or the newscasters, the Animal Rights people, the rangers or the zoo-keeper, Mr. Fortney, or even the Conroys had arrived.

The grass on the soccer field was trampled and muddy. The yellow keep-back tape looked as if a herd of elephants had marched across it.

Edward hurried along the path that went around the lake. In his mind, he could see the spot where Rooter's shadow had appeared on the TV screen, right near a bush that looked like a camel with one hump.

As soon as he spotted the bush, Edward slowed down and, practicing his Indian hunting walk, he moved quietly toward it.

But Rooter wasn't there. And Edward couldn't find any sign that he ever had been. Edward put his hands around his mouth, so his voice would carry. "Here, Rooter," he called. "Here, boy."

No Rooter.

Disappointed, Edward continued along the path, grumpily kicking a small stone ahead of him as he went. "Here, Rooter," he called again.

Then he saw the alligator.

This time it wasn't hiding in the reeds or cautiously sliding into the water. This time, as if it didn't have an enemy in the world, the alligator was playing. It was playing a game with drops of water falling out of an irrigation pipe into the lake.

First the alligator stalked the pipe, stealthily sneaking up on it. Then it snapped at the drops of water. Then it closed its jaws, tilted its head up, and let the drops fall onto its snout. Then it smiled.

Edward slid down the grassy slope by the side of the lake and got as close as he dared. He got so interested in watching the alligator play he forgot about all the rest. He forgot about alligator catchers. He forgot about animal rights. He forgot about

Rooter. He sat perfectly still and watched until the alligator finished playing, swam out into deeper water, and submerged.

Then Edward had the feeling there was someone on the path above him. He turned quickly and looked up. Standing there was a figure wearing boots, blue jeans, and—brightly shining in the morning sun—an alligator belt buckle.

Shading her eyes with her hand, Earline Hooke gazed intently out at the water. Edward's envious eyes gazed intently at the gleaming brass buckle.

Finally, after she had finished examining every inch of the lake, Earline turned her eyes to the shore. "Hey," she said when she saw Edward.

"Hi," Edward replied. How much had she seen, he wondered.

Earline looked as if she was making up her mind about something. Then she slid down and sat next to Edward.

"Whatcha' doin'?" she asked. Edward took his time answering. "Whatcha' doin'?" she repeated, in a way that let Edward know she would keep asking until she got an answer.

"Looking for something," Edward said.

"For what?"

"A dog."

"A dog? Are you sure?"

"Of course I'm sure. I'm looking for a dog named Rooter. An old dog that's lost. What are you doing?"

Edward tried to tell from Earline's expression whether she had or hadn't seen the baby alligator playing with the drops of water. Earline wasn't smiling. She looked serious. And she looked worried. She hadn't seen it, Edward decided.

"What I'm doin' is lookin' for the 'gator," Earline answered with a sigh.

"Oh, yeah, the 'gator. I wonder if it's still around," Edward bluffed.

"I saw it yesterday," Earline reminded him.

"Yesterday's not the same as today," said Edward.

"Thanks for the late-breakin' news," Earline replied. "What's your name?"

"Edward," he said.

"Come again?"

"Edward," he repeated loudly. "Edward Fraser."

"You don't have to shout, Edward."

"Sorry."

"Never mind. I'm Earline Hooke."

"I know that," said Edward. "Everybody in the world knows that."

Earline looked pleased. Then she scanned the

lake again. "What makes you think this dog you're lookin' for is around here?" she asked finally.

"I thought I saw him, last night on TV," Edward explained. "I thought I saw him right near that bush." He pointed in the general direction of the bush with his chin.

"Over there?" asked Earline, nodding toward some tangled shrubbery.

"No," Edward said, "the one over there that's shaped like a camel." Rats and gnats, Edward thought. He'd done it again. Now Earline Hooke was going to have something to say about his darn imagination.

But Earline surprised him. She looked carefully around until she spotted the right bush. "That one?" she asked. "That one over there that looks like a one-humped camel?"

"That's it," said Edward. "How could you tell?"

"I've got a lively imagination," Earline explained.

"You do?"

"I do," she repeated. "You might say it's one of my best features. Granddaddy brags on it all the time."

"He brags about your imagination?" Edward marveled. "He thinks it's good?"

" 'Course he thinks it's good," Earline replied. "It

*is* good. Imagination's one of the best things a person can have. It's what lets you think of things nobody else has thought of."

"I always thought imagination just really meant lies," admitted Edward.

Earline gave that some thought. "Well, yes," she said. "A good liar would have to be someone with a good imagination. What's wrong with that?"

"What's wrong with lying?"

"Well, there's lyin' and then there's lyin'," Earline explained. "There's babyish little lies that anybody can see through. And then there's mean old lies that hurt people. But then there's other lies—the kind of lies that make good stories, f'r instance. That's the kind of lie I mean, the kind that's the same as imagination."

"You think it's good to lie?" Edward asked.

"Naw," Earline said impatiently. "I think it's good to have plenty of imagination. Isn't that what I just got through explainin'?"

"Well, yes," Edward admitted, "but—"

"But nothin'," interrupted Earline. "Looky, I don't have time to just sit here jawin'. I've got to locate that blamed 'gator so I can help my granddaddy."

"Help him how?" Edward asked.

"By catchin' it for him, of course."

Edward gazed into the distance. He tried to look as if he didn't care what Earline's answer was. "Catching it?" he asked.

"Rescuin' it, I mean," she said.

Edward looked back at Earline. He stuck his face up close to hers. "Well, which is it?" he demanded.

"Rescue!" she yelled.

"You don't have to shout," said Edward, backing off. "I was just asking."

"Sorry," said Earline. "Just, everythin's been so peculiar since Granddaddy and I got here. I've got me a short fuse now, is all."

"Short fuse?"

"I'm short-tempered. In a bad mood. And impatient." Earline was raising her voice. She caught herself. "Sorry," she said again.

"Things have been peculiar?" Edward prompted. "What things?"

"Every dad-blamed thing," Earline swore. "Everythin's been peculiar, everybody's been weird, and every single thing that's happened to us has been bad. I regret that Granddaddy and I ever came up here to try to help with your dern alligator."

"Sorry," Edward mumbled.

"You don't have to apologize," Earline replied. "It's not your fault."

Edward was silent. He examined the toes of his sneakers. "Well, it sort of is my fault," he said at last. "I'm the one who saw the alligator in the first place."

"You?" asked Earline. Edward nodded. "Well then, it is your fault," she decided. "And you owe us."

"Owe you?"

"You owe Granddaddy and me. If you hadn't of seen the 'gator, we wouldn't be here. And Granddaddy wouldn't be laid up with two sprained wrists and a twisted ankle. And made a fool of, besides."

"I said I was sorry," Edward reminded her.

"Sorry's not good enough," Earline informed him. "Sorry won't do. Not when Captain Jim-Bob Hooke has been humiliated."

"Humiliated?" asked Edward.

"Embarrassed and made to look a fool, like I said," replied Earline.

"But what can I do except apologize?" Edward asked.

"Well," said Earline, "you could help me figure out how to find the 'gator. That'd go a long way toward helpin' me to catch it."

Edward pounced. "Catch?"

"Rescue," Earline shot back.

"Well, which is it?" Edward demanded.

"What difference does it make?" Earline asked.

"It makes a difference," insisted Edward. "It makes a difference to me."

Earline gave in. "Well, in this case, it's rescue," she allowed.

"Really?"

"Yep. If it was some regular outlaw 'gator down home, some troublesome crittur ten or twelve foot long, we'd be talkin' 'catch.'

"But this pipsqueak 'gator y'all have got up here? We're talkin' 'rescue.' The whole idea is to get it to a warmer climate and into warmer water, so it won't get sick and die."

Edward was listening closely.

"There's a wildlife preserve in Louisiana that'll take it off our hands, once we—rescue—it. They'll keep it in a holdin' pool for a couple of months, and then they'll turn it loose so it can go live in the swamps with the other 'gators."

Edward pounced again. "And then you or somebody else will try to catch it! Right?"

"Wrong!" Earline pounced back. "Unless it grows up to be an outlaw, that is."

Edward thought about the baby alligator playing its game with the drops of water. He knew it would never be an outlaw.

"Well," he decided, "since it really is 'rescue,' I'll help."

Earline didn't seem as pleased as he thought she would. "Okay," she said. "How?"

"How?" said Edward. "How should I know how? You're the alligator expert, aren't you?"

"Of course not," she answered. "Granddaddy's the expert, not me. If I was the expert, I wouldn't need help, would I?"

Edward hesitated. "I guess not," he allowed.

"So how?" Earline repeated.

"Let me think," Edward said.

They both were quiet while Edward frowned and squinted and hit his head with his fist, making it clear how hard he was thinking.

"I know!" he said. "We could get a clock, and we could get the alligator to swallow it. And then we'd always know where it was because the clock inside it would be going tick-tick, and you'd be able to rescue it anytime you wanted to. What do you think of that?"

For a moment, Earline seemed interested. Then

she shook her head. "Naw," she said, "wouldn' work."

"Why not?"

"Well, for one thing, clocks don't go tick-tock anymore."

"Tick-tick," interrupted Edward.

Earline gave him a steely look. "Tick-*tock*," she insisted. Then she went on. "Nobody's got a clock like that. Nowadays clocks run on batteries. Clocks are quiet. Even if we could get the 'gator to swallow a clock, it wouldn' help a bit.

"Anyway, if I knew where the crittur was, I wouldn' waste time tryin' to get it to swallow somethin'. I'd just—rescue it."

Edward knew Earline was right. All the Frasers' clocks ran on batteries. All of them were quiet. Not a single clock in the house made any noise at all.

Earline stood up. Her alligator buckle was about even with Edward's eyes. He gazed greedily at it. "I gotta go," she said.

"No!" Edward cried, scrambling to his feet. "I mean, wait a minute. I've got another idea!"

Earline was doubtful. "You do?"

"Really, I do," Edward assured her, looking at her with his most honest expression.

"Well, what's your idea?"

Edward, bedazzled by the buckle, could hardly think.

Impatient, Earline put her hands on her hips and leaned over him. "Well?" she demanded.

"What if I told you I saw the alligator this morning, right before you came?" said Edward.

"What if I told you the moon was made of Swiss cheese?" replied Earline.

Edward thought. "I wouldn't believe you," he decided.

"Right," Earline said. "That's what I meant."

"What?" asked Edward.

"I meant I don't believe you!" Earline shouted.

"You don't need to yell," Edward said.

"Sorry," muttered Earline. Then, "*Did* you see it this mornin'?"

"Yep," Edward said. "I saw it right over there, playing." He pointed to the irrigation pipe and to the drops of water falling one by one into the lake.

"Playin'?" Earline asked. "What do you mean, playin'?"

"It was playing a game it made up."

"The alligator was playin' a game it made up," repeated Earline. "Sure it was."

"It was," Edward insisted. "It was playing with

the drops of water falling out of that pipe. It was sneaking up on them and snapping at them. It was letting them drip on its face. And it was smiling."

Earline shook her head disapprovingly at Edward. "Do you really expect me to believe that?" she asked.

Edward scratched the back of his neck. "I guess not," he answered sadly.

"Chee, you really have got some imagination," said Earline.

Edward sighed. "Yeah," he said.

Now Earline looked shrewdly at Edward. "But you did see the alligator today, didn't you?" she guessed.

Edward looked shrewdly at Earline. "Maybe," he said.

"Maybe you've seen it?" she asked.

"Maybe I'll tell you."

"Tell me whether you've seen it?"

"Yep," said shrewd Edward.

"And where you've seen it?" said shrewd Earline.

"Yep. If . . ." said Edward.

"If . . . ?" asked Earline.

Edward stared meaningfully at the alligator buckle. The buckle winked in the sun.

"If . . ." Earline said.

"If you . . ." Edward coached.

"If I . . ."

"If you let me wear your . . ." prompted Edward.

"If I let you wear my alligator buckle?" she said. Edward nodded. "You'll tell me where you really saw the 'gator this mornin' if I let you wear my belt buckle?" asked Earline.

Shrewd Edward nodded. He could feel the heavy buckle tugging on the front of his own belt. He could imagine himself swaggering down the street with the brass alligator winking in the sun.

"Why would I part with my alligator buckle to try to find out where the 'gator was this mornin'?" asked the frustrated girl. "I need to know where the alligator's goin' to be tomorrow mornin', so I can get it rescued and Granddaddy and I can go home!"

Edward felt the heavy brass buckle slip off his belt. "I can tell you where the alligator is every morning!" he cried. "Honest!"

"Where, then?" demanded Earline, studying Edward's face. Was he telling her the truth, or was he trying to trick her with another lie?

Edward looked at Earline, truth written all over him. He knew where the alligator had been that morning. And he was absolutely sure he knew where the alligator would be tomorrow morning. The alligator would be right over there, under the irrigation pipe, playing.

"Where?" she repeated.

"Right over there, playing with the drops of water," Edward said, feeling every bit as truthful as he looked.

"Over there!" sputtered Earline.

"Yep, right over there, playing with the water coming out of that pipe. Just like this morning."

"Hold on now," Earline said, "it wasn't over there doin' that this mornin'. That was somethin' you made up, remember? You told me you made it up!"

"No, you told me I made it up," Edward reminded her. "You asked me if I expected you to believe it. And I said no. But I never said I made it up."

Earline's face turned red, then redder. "You really did see the 'gator over there this mornin'?" she asked finally.

Truthful Edward nodded. "Yes," he said.

"And that's where the 'gator is, real early every mornin'?" Earline asked.

Truthful Edward nodded again.

"Are you sure?"

Edward was sure.

"Okay, then," Earline decided. "Meet me right back here at daybreak tomorrow. If the 'gator's here, and if we get it, you can wear my belt buckle for two whole hours. Deal?"

"Deal!" agreed Edward. "But how are we going to do it?"

"Well, we'll need Granddaddy's fishin' pole and the heavy line and the 'gator hook. I can bring those. And we'll need a big empty carton to plop down over it after I hook it and drag it ashore."

"We have a big carton out in our garage," Edward offered. "It's my brother Jason's and mine. We used to play with it all the time. We pretended it was a spaceship and a diving bell and a cabin in the woods and . . ."

"Edward?" Earline interrupted.

"Yes?"

"Just tell me, can you bring that carton and meet me here at dawn tomorrow or not?"

"I can," Edward promised.

"Okay," said Earline. "Be here. With your spaceship. And . . ."

"Spaceship?" Edward interrupted.

"I mean the box," said Earline. "Be here with the box. And don't tell anybody what we're goin' to do."

"Why not?"

" 'Cause if they knew, they'd prob'ly try and stop us."

"Why?"

"Oh," Earline said airily, "you know how some people are. They'd say it was too dangerous for a couple of kids to rescue a little ol' 'gator." She paused. "Silly, huh?"

"Hunh," agreed Edward.

"Pardon?" said Earline.

"I mean, huh," Edward said. "Really silly."

"Right. So no point in tellin' and givin' them a chance to get in our way, right?"

"Right," agreed Edward.

"So you're not goin' to tell anyone."

"Right," agreed Edward.

"Shake on it," said Earline, putting out her hand.

Edward hesitated. "You don't think it *is* too dangerous, do you?" he asked.

"Naw," said Earline. "Do you think I'd let you help me if it was?"

Edward thought.

"C'mon, Edward," Earline coaxed. "Would I?"

Edward thought some more.

"And don't forget, after we do the job, this here's

yours for two whole hours." She pointed to the thrashing brass alligator.

"It's not too dangerous," Edward decided. He shook Earline's hand. "I won't tell."

Edward and Earline left the park separately, just in case. And Edward got almost all the way home before he realized that he really couldn't be sure where the alligator would be the next morning.

# Hunh?

On Friday morning, something woke Jason before it was time to get up. And he wasn't just half awake. He was wide awake. He tried closing his eyes, but they popped back open. So he lay in his bed, listening. All he could hear were the birds beginning to call to one another and the sound of his and Edward's pet rats running in their exercise wheels. He turned over and pulled the comforter around his shoulders. Then he tried closing his eyes again. Again, they popped open. Obesity and bunions! he swore to himself. That was something Captain Hook said in the play of *Peter Pan*. Jason liked the sound of it. He lay there until he heard the front door carefully closing. Edward! he thought. What was going on?

Quickly Jason got up and scrambled into the clothes he'd worn the day before, which were crumpled conveniently there on the floor right next to his bed. In the kitchen, he saw the same note that had been there yesterday morning. "I am looking for Rooter," the note said. "Love, Edward Fraser."

Jason slipped out the front door and closed it quietly behind him. He looked around. There in the driveway was Edward, wrestling with the large cardboard carton from their garage. He was trying to figure out how to carry it. First he held it in front of him. Then to one side. Then to the other. Any way he held it, even though it was empty and not very heavy, it was awkward when he tried to walk.

Jason almost laughed out loud, but he caught himself. Then he slipped behind the hedge and hightailed it to the other end of the driveway, where he waited for Edward. Here he came, balancing the carton on top of his head and steadying it with his hands.

"Hi, Edward," Jason said.

Edward jumped a mile. The carton slipped and fell to the ground. "Jason!" he croaked.

"Where are you going?" Jason asked.

"To the park. I mean, to look for Rooter—um—at the park."

"What's the box for?"

"The box?" Edward looked at the big carton lying on its side at his feet as if he'd never laid eyes on it before.

"The box," Jason said. "That box. The one you were carrying on your head a minute ago."

"Right," said Edward. "The box. I'm—I'm going to throw it over Rooter when I find him, so he can't get away—I mean, so he can't get lost again."

"You're going to throw a box over Rooter? Edward, that's ridiculous." Edward looked down. "Let's start again," Jason suggested. "Edward, where are you going with that?"

"I don't have time to start again, Jason," Edward pleaded. "I have to go. It's getting late."

"Late?" Jason asked. "You call this 'late'?"

"I mean *I'm* late, Jason."

"Late for what?"

"For meeting someone," Edward explained. "For meeting someone who's going to help me catch—I mean rescue—Rooter."

Jason thought for a moment. "Edward," he decided, "you're lying."

"I'm not lying, Jas," Edward protested. "I *am* going to the park. I *am* meeting someone. And I *am* late. I've got to go."

"Okay," Jason said pleasantly. "I'll go with you. I'll help you carry the box."

"You don't have to do that, Jason, honest. I can do it myself."

"Sure you can. But I'm up, and I'm dressed, and it's too early to do anything because everyone else in the world is asleep. So I might as well go with you to the park and help you rescue old Rooter."

"Gee, Jason," Edward said, "that's really nice of you. But you don't have to. I mean, it's not too early to do anything. You could have breakfast and read the paper. Or you could go back to sleep. Or you could—"

"If you're late already, we better go," Jason interrupted.

He picked up one side of the box and motioned to Edward to get the other side.

"Who are you meeting, anyway?" Jason asked.

"Someone," Edward said.

Jason stopped walking and put down his side of the box. "Who?" he demanded.

"Someone you don't know," Edward stalled.

"Named?"

Edward thought.

"The person's name? The one you're going to meet at the park?" encouraged Jason.

Edward studied his sneakers. "Earline Hooke," he said.

"Earline Hooke? Earline Hooke is helping you look for Rooter?"

Edward nodded.

"Wait a minute. I wasn't born yesterday," said Jason.

Edward laughed. "I know that, Jas."

"What I mean is, I'm not as easy to fool as a newborn baby," said Jason.

Edward was indignant. "Did someone say you were?"

Jason took a deep breath. "Let's try to stay on track here, Edward," he said. "You're going to the park to meet Earline Hooke to help her try to catch the alligator, aren't you?"

Edward looked brightly up at his brother. "That's a really good idea, Jas," he bluffed. "Why didn't I think of that? After we catch Rooter, we can try to get the alligator!"

"Stop that, Edward," Jason commanded. "You're

going there now to try to catch the alligator, right?"

"Wrong," Edward said.

"Wrong? Are you sure?"

"Yes, I'm sure."

"Then what are you and Earline Hooke really going to the park to do? And quit trying to sell me that Rooter story. I'm not buying."

"And I'm not selling," Edward cracked, "I'm giving it to you for free!"

"Edward . . ." warned Jason.

"Well, we are not going to try to catch the alligator."

"Are you sure?" said Jason.

"Of course I'm sure. I would never help Earline catch the alligator. I'm going to help her *rescue* the alligator."

Jason was silent.

"What are you going to do, Jason? Are you going to tell?"

Jason was still silent. "No," he said finally. "I'm not going to tell. I'm going to go with you." He picked up his side of the carton. "Come on."

"That's okay, Jason," Edward assured him. "I can do it by myself."

"Okay," Jason said. Relieved, Edward picked up

the big box, put it on his head, and set off again. Jason walked at his side.

"I thought you were staying home, Jason," Edward said.

"What made you think that?"

"You said so."

"Nope, I didn't," Jason said.

"You did, Jas. You said okay, and you let me carry the box by myself."

"But I never said I wasn't coming with you. Do you think I'd let you do something as stupid as this without me?"

Edward wasn't sure whether Jason was insulting him or not.

When Edward got tired of balancing the carton on his head, he and Jason went back to carrying it together. That's what they were doing when Janice Conroy, following her nose for news, caught sight of them and decided to tail them. And that's what she was doing when her sisters, Marlene and Marilyn, ever watchful and enterprising, began to follow her.

Through the still-sleeping neighborhood they went, Edward and Jason awkwardly walking with the box; Janice Conroy, girl reporter, staying behind but keeping them in sight; Marlene and Mari-

lyn, red-faced from the effort of keeping quiet and trying not to walk too fast and catch up.

Into Shaw Park Edward and Jason went, across the soccer field, and around to the far side of Shaw Park Lake.

"We're here." Edward put down his side of the box. Jason put down his. It was so early, mist was still rising off the water, and not another soul was in sight. Not even Earline Hooke was there. And beneath the dripping irrigation pipe, no alligator.

"Now what?" Jason wanted to know.

Edward shrugged. "We have to wait for Earline," he said.

"What if she doesn't come?" Jason asked. Edward shrugged again. "Well, do we throw the box over the alligator ourselves?" Jason persisted. "If we can find it, that is."

Edward hadn't thought of that. It sounded like a good idea to him. But it wasn't part of the plan. And he wasn't sure it would work, even if the alligator did show itself. Besides, it would probably mean he wouldn't get to wear the alligator buckle.

Suddenly Edward felt confused. He began to think about school. He began to think about orderly, organized days. School would be starting again on Monday. He could hardly wait.

The boys stood on the path with their carton. Janice Conroy concealed herself behind a tree and took out her pen and her reporter's notebook. Marlene and Marilyn hushed each other and hid together behind some bushes, peering through the foliage.

They all waited.

Finally, Earline Hooke arrived, breathless from hurrying, holding her granddaddy's fishing pole with the three-pronged alligator hook strung to one end of the line.

Jason stepped behind the box and hunkered down. Edward wanted to know why, but before he could ask, there was Earline.

"Hey," she said.

"Hi," Edward replied.

"Did you remember to say 'Rabbit rabbit' first thing when you woke up this mornin' for good luck? I did."

"Sure I did," Edward fibbed. He'd never heard of this before, but he didn't want Earline to think it was his fault if they didn't have good luck.

"Good," said Earline.

"You're late," Edward noted.

Just then Jason stood up. Earline stared hard at him. "Who's this?" she demanded.

"It's my brother, Jason," replied Edward. "He said 'Rabbit rabbit' first thing this morning, too."

"He did?" Earline said. "How come? What did you tell him?"

"I—I didn't tell him anything. Honest, I didn't. He—he always says 'Rabbit rabbit' first thing in the morning. For good luck. In case he needs it later. He's a careful kind of person. Right, Jason?"

"What's he doin' here, Edward? Who else did you tell? And where's the 'gator?" said Earline.

"He came to help," answered Edward, "and I didn't tell anyone else. I didn't even tell him. And—what's the other question?"

"The other question is, where's the 'gator? You said the 'gator would be here playin'. You said he was here every mornin'."

"I did?" said Edward.

"You know you did!"

"Keep it down," said Jason. "If the alligator's anywhere near, you'll scare it off."

Earline knew he was right. She stage-whispered,

"Does the alligator play here every mornin', Edward, or doesn't it? Am I wastin' my time or not?"

"Yes," said Edward.

"I am?" she hollered.

"Shhhh," said Jason.

"I mean, no," said Edward.

"What? The alligator doesn't come here every mornin'?" cried Earline. "You said you *knew* it did!"

Jason took over. "Try to be calm," he said. "Edward means yes, the alligator usually is here. And no, you're not wasting your time. He was answering your questions in order. Right, Edward?" Edward nodded. "Now," Jason continued, "what's the plan?"

Earline looked suspiciously at Jason. She fiddled with the alligator hook, to make sure it was tied securely. She looked intently out over the water. Finally, she answered. "This here 'gator," she said, "leastwise, accordin' to your brother, who has an imagination to beat all—" She stopped talking and glared at Edward. Edward looked up at the sky. "Accordin' to your brother, who is basically a liar—"

Jason held up his hand. "I can't let you call my brother a liar, Earline," he said.

"Well, that's what he is," she replied.

"I know that," said Jason, "but I can't let you say so."

"Why not, if it's true?" Earline wanted to know.

"Yeah, Jas," Edward asked, "why not?"

"It would be wrong for me to let someone call you a liar, Edward."

"But Jason, you call me a liar all the time!" said Edward.

"Edward," Earline explained, "that's entirely different. Your own brother can call you anythin' he wants. But a stranger can't."

Jason backed her up. "She's right, Edward. I'm surprised you have to have that explained."

"Wait a minute, Jason, whose side are you on, anyway?" cried Edward.

"On your side," Jason replied angrily.

"He's on your side, dum-dum," Earline added.

"And don't call him dum-dum," Jason said.

"Would you two quit arguing and picking on me and get to the point!" said Edward.

"What point?" Jason and Earline asked.

"The plan," said Edward. "Jason asked you about the plan."

"Oh, right," said Earline. "Well, as I was sayin', your brother says the 'gator plays with the drops of water comin' out of that pipe. Every mornin', he says." She paused to frown a warning frown at Edward. "So I figured, when the crittur was busy playin', I'd cast out this here line and hook it."

"Where would you be?"

"Right here." Earline walked to a position about fifteen feet away from the irrigation pipe.

"Then what?" asked Jason.

"Then I'd haul it up onto the shore. And Edward would be down there waitin' to slap the box down over the 'gator and lean on it while I skiddoo and get us some help."

"Edward's going to be down there with the alligator while you go for help?" said Jason.

Earline got his point. "Well," she said, "we could do it the other way around. Edward could cast the line and get that hook into the 'gator and run for help, and I could hold down the box."

"I couldn't do that, Earline," Edward said.

"I know it," replied the girl.

"She's just being sarcastic," Jason translated.

"Hmmph," remarked Earline.

Just then, Marlene Conroy stood up. "Here it comes!" she cried. Marilyn Conroy stood up. "Where?" she wanted to know.

Then Janice Conroy stood up. "What are you two doing here?" she demanded.

Earline, Jason, and Edward gaped at the Conroys.

And before anyone could say anything more, another voice surprised them all. It was the voice of Captain Jim-Bob Hooke. "What in tarnation is goin' on here?" the Captain boomed.

Captain Hooke hobbled over to Earline. One of his wrists was in a sling and the other one was bound with an Ace bandage.

"Earline Hollyberry Hooke," he said, "what're you doin' down here with my gear?"

Before Earline could answer him, Marilyn Conroy spoke again. "There it is!" she said softly.

They all looked. There was the alligator, stealthily stalking the drops of water as they fell from the irrigation pipe into the lake.

They watched it play the same game Edward had seen the day before. First it stalked the drops. Then it snapped at them. Then it closed its eyes and lifted its head so the drops of water dripped onto its snout. And then it smiled.

But suddenly everything changed. A fishing line came flying through the air and the three-pronged hook on the end of it snagged the alligator's tough

hide down near its tail. With eyes and mouth wide open in surprise, the alligator was pulled backwards into deeper water.

The park rangers, out in a small rowboat, trying to find the alligator before all the hoopla started up again, had hooked it with a three-pronged alligator hook Captain Hooke had given them.

Now one ranger rowed toward the opposite shore while the other held on to the fishing pole. The alligator tried to swim forward. But the hook held.

When they reached the shore, one ranger climbed out of the boat and took the pole from the other. Then he gently reeled the alligator in and pulled it into the dog kennel they had waiting. The sound the kennel door made as they closed it echoed around Shaw Park Lake.

The alligator was rescued.

Janice Conroy rushed over to Captain Hooke. "Captain, how do you feel about having your alligator rescued by somebody else?" she asked, her pen ready to write down his answer in her reporter's notebook.

Marilyn and Marlene crowded in behind Janice, eager to hear every word. Earline stepped to her grandfather's side. Edward and Jason stood wide-eyed by the empty box.

"Wal, I don't rightly think of it as my 'gator, little lady," said Captain Hooke politely.

"It isn't his 'gator," Earline reminded Janice. "It's y'all's 'gator. Granddaddy's only here to help. And he has. He gave the park rangers one of his special alligator hooks, and he told them how to use it. Mission accomplished. Wouldn' you say?"

Janice was busy writing. But Marlene and Marilyn were suspicious.

"What are Jason and Edward doing here?" Marlene asked.

"And how come they're looking so guilty?" Marilyn wanted to know.

"Guilty?" cried Jason. "Who's looking guilty?"

"You and Edward, that's who," replied Marlene.

"Me and Edward?" Jason was incredulous. "What in the world would we have to look guilty about?"

"That's what we want to find out," said Marilyn.

"Exactly!" agreed Marlene.

"Huhn," grumbled Edward.

"Huhn?" said Captain Hooke.

"Huh?" said Jason and Earline.

"Stop that, all of you," said Janice. "I've got a job

to finish here." Everyone was silent. She turned back to the Hookes. "Now," she said, "what's your next step, Captain?"

"I intend to catch the next plane out of here, little lady," answered Captain Hooke. "We'd like to get home just as quick as we can. Right, honey?"

"Right, Granddaddy."

Captain Hooke hobbled toward the path on his hurt ankle. Earline followed him.

They were going home. And they were taking their shiny, alligator-encrusted belt buckles with them.

"Earline!" cried Edward.

Earline turned and shrugged. "I gotta go," she said. "Sorry."

"I just meant—goodbye," he fibbed.

Earline grinned at him. "I know that," she fibbed back. " 'Bye!"

# Ducks

On Sunday, the last day of his spring vacation, Edward rode his bike to Shaw Park Lake.

Everything was the way it was supposed to be. Old Rooter had turned up the day before, and now he was fast asleep in the middle of the street, with his gray muzzle resting on his paws.

At the park, the men were playing Go and chess.

The sandbox was full of toddlers.

The turtles were lined up one behind another on their log.

The swans were gliding through the water.

The cantankerous goose was patrolling the shore.

And, out for a peaceful swim was a familiar-looking family of ducks—a father, a mother, and six fluffy brown babies.

Six?

Six!